Quiz No 202923
I Was a Rat!

Pullman, Philip
B.L.: 5.2
Points: 4.0

MY

I WAS A RAT!

...or *The Scarlet Slippers*

Also by Philip Pullman

I WAS A RAT!

...or *The Scarlet Slippers*

PHILIP PULLMAN

Illustrated by Peter Bailey

DOUBLEDAY

London • New York • Toronto • Sydney • Auckland

This story is for Jack, Kate and Rosie

TRANSWORLD PUBLISHERS LTD
61–63 Uxbridge Road, London W5 5SA

TRANSWORLD PUBLISHERS, C/O RANDOM HOUSE (AUSTRALIA) PTY LTD
20 Alfred Street, Milsons Point, NSW 2061, Australia

TRANSWORLD PUBLISHERS, C/O RANDOM HOUSE (NZ) LTD
18 Poland Road, Glenfield, Auckland, New Zealand

DOUBLEDAY CANADA LTD
105 Bond Street, Toronto, Ontario M5B 1Y3

Published in 1999 by Doubleday
a division of Transworld Publishers Ltd

A catalogue record for this book is available from the British Library

ISBN 0 385 409796

Typeset by Falcon Oast Graphic Art, East Hoathly
Printed in Great Britain
by Mackays plc, Chatham, Kent

The Daily Scourge

LOVE AT THE BALL

by our Court Correspondent

Yes – it's official!

Hunky Prince Richard has found a bride at last!

At midnight last night, the Palace announced the engagement of His Royal Highness Prince Richard to the Lady Aurelia Ashington.

'We are very happy,' said the Prince.

It is understood that the Royal Wedding will be celebrated very soon.

Our Romance Correspondent writes:

It was like something out of a fairy tale. The charming prince, the mysterious girl who seemed to vanish into nowhere only to be found by the merest chance . . .

They met at the Midsummer Ball. To the music of a shimmering waltz, they danced like thistledown, and they only had eyes for each other.

'I've never seen him so in love,' said a close friend of the Prince. 'I think this time it's the real thing.'

It was certainly fast. By midnight, they were head over heels in love, and it only took another day for the engagement to be made official.

PRINCE RICHARD – THE LOVER

A fact-file of the playboy prince's previous girlfriends – *page 2,3,4,5,6,7,8*

LADY AURELIA – WHERE DOES SHE COME FROM?

Our reporters investigate the background of the lovely young Princess-to-be – *page 9*

Stars in their eyes!

I Was A Rat!

O ld Bob and his wife Joan lived by the market in the house where his father and grand-father and great-grandfather had lived before him, cobblers all of them, and cobbling was Bob's trade too. Joan was a washerwoman, like her mother and her grandmother and her great-grandmother, back as far as anyone could remember.

And if they'd had a son, he would have become a cobbler in his turn, and if they'd had a daughter, she would have learned the laundry trade, and so the world would have gone on. But they never had a child, whether boy or girl, and now they were get-ting old, it seemed less and less likely that they ever would, much as they would have liked to.

One evening as old Joan wrote a letter to her niece and old Bob sat trimming the heels of a pair

of tiny scarlet slippers he was making for the love of it, there came a knock at the door.

Bob looked up with a jump. 'Was that someone knocking?' he said. 'What's the time?'

The cuckoo clock answered him before Joan could: ten o'clock. As soon as it had finished cuckooing, there came another knock, louder than before.

Bob lit a candle and went through the dark shop to unlock the front door.

Standing in the moonlight was a little boy in a page's uniform. It had once been smart, but it was sorely torn and stained, and the boy's face was scratched and grubby.

'Bless my soul!' said Bob. 'Who are you?'

'I was a rat,' said the little boy.

'What did you say?' said Joan, crowding in behind her husband.

'I was a rat,' said the little boy again.

'You were a – go on with you! Where do you live?' she said. 'What's your name?'

But the little boy could only say, 'I was a rat.'

The old couple took him into the kitchen, because the

night was cold, and sat him down by the fire. He looked at the flames as if he'd never seen anything like them before.

'What should we do?' whispered Bob.

'Feed the poor little soul,' Joan whispered back. 'Bread and milk, that's what my mother used to make for us.'

So she put some milk in a pan to heat by the fire and broke some bread into a bowl, and old Bob tried to find out more about the boy.

'What's your name?' he said.

'Haven't got a name.'

'Why, everyone's got a name! I'm Bob, and this is Joan, and that's who we are, see. You sure you haven't got a name?'

'I lost it. I forgot it. I was a rat,' said the boy, as if that explained everything.

'Oh,' said Bob. 'You got a nice uniform on, anyway. I expect you're in service, are you?'

The boy looked at his tattered uniform, puzzled.

'Dunno,' he said finally. 'Dunno what that means. I expect I am, probably.'

'In service,' said Bob, 'that means being someone's servant. Have a master or a mistress and run errands for 'em. Page-boys, like you, they usually go along with the master or mistress in a coach, for instance.'

'Ah,' said the boy. 'Yes, I done that, I was a good page-boy, I done everything right.'

'Course you did,' said Bob, shifting his chair along as Joan came to the table with the bowl of warm bread and milk.

She put it in front of the boy and without a second's pause he put his face right down into the bowl and began to guzzle it up directly, his dirty little hands gripping the edge of the table.

'What you doing?' said Joan. 'Dear oh dear! You don't eat like that. Use the spoon!'

The boy looked up, milk in his eyebrows, bread up his nose, his chin dripping.

'He doesn't know anything, poor little thing,' said Joan. 'Come to the sink, my love, and we'll wash you. Grubby hands and all. Look at you!'

The boy tried to look at himself, but he was reluctant to leave the bowl.

'That's nice,' he said. 'I like that . . .'

'It'll still be here when you come back,' said Bob. 'I've had my supper already, I'll look after it for you.'

The boy looked wonder-struck at this idea. He watched over his shoulder as Joan led him to the kitchen sink and tipped in some water from the kettle, and while she was washing him he kept twisting his wet face round to look from Bob to the bowl and back again.

'That's better,' said Joan, rubbing him dry. 'Now you be a good boy and eat with the spoon.'

'Yes, I will,' he said, nodding.

'I'm surprised they didn't teach you manners when you was a page-boy,' she said.

'I was a rat,' he said.

'Oh, well, rats don't have manners. Boys do,' she told him. 'You say thank you when someone gives you something, see, that's good manners.'

'Thank you,' he said, nodding hard.

'That's a good boy. Now come and sit down.'

So he sat down, and Bob showed him how to use the spoon. He found it hard at first, because he would keep turning it upside down before it reached his mouth, and a lot of the bread and milk ended up on his lap.

But Bob and Joan could see he was trying, and he was a quick learner. By the time he'd finished, he was quite good at it.

'Thank you,' he said.

'That's it. Well done,' said Bob. 'Now you come along with me and I'll show you how to wash the bowl and the spoon.' While they were doing that, Bob said, 'D'you know how old you are?'

'Yes,' said the boy. 'I know that all right. I'm three weeks old, I am.'

'Three weeks?'

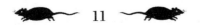

11

'Yes. And I got two brothers and two sisters, the same age, three weeks.'

'Five of you?'

'Yes. I ain't seen 'em for a long time.'

'What's a long time?'

The boy thought, and said, 'Days.'

'And where's your mother and father?'

'Under the ground.'

Bob and Joan looked at each other, and they could each see what the other was feeling. The poor little boy was an orphan, and grief had turned his mind, and he'd wandered away from the orphanage he must have been living in.

As it happened, on the table beside him was Bob's newspaper, and suddenly the little boy seemed to see it for the first time.

'Here!' he said, delighted. 'That's Mary Jane!'

He was pointing to a picture of the Prince's new fiancée. The Prince had met her just the other day and they'd fallen in love at once, and the royal engagement was the main story of the week.

'She's going to marry the Prince,' said Bob, 'but she ain't called Mary Jane. That ain't the kind of name they give princesses.'

'I expect you must have got confused,' said Joan. 'And you can't go anywhere else tonight, that's for sure. We'll make you up a bed, my love, and you can sleep here, and we'll find the proper place for you in the morning.'

'Ah,' he said. 'I didn't know that proper place, else I'd have gone there tonight.'

'Look, we'll have to call you something,' said Bob.

'Something,' the boy said, as if he was memorising it.

'A proper name,' said Joan. 'Like . . . Kaspar. Or . . .'

'Crispin,' said Bob. 'He's the saint of shoemakers, he is. That's a good name.'

'I bet there's a saint of washerwomen, too,' said Joan. 'Only no-one's ever heard of her.'

'Well, if it's a her, it'd be no good as a name for him, would it?'

'No, probably not,' she said. 'I don't suppose . . . I don't suppose we could call him Roger, could we?'

Roger was the name they would have called a son of their own, if they'd ever had one.

'It's only for tonight,' said Bob. 'Can't do any harm.'

'Little boy,' said Joan, touching his shoulder. 'We got to call you by a name, and if you ain't got one of your own, we'll call you Roger.'

'Yes,' said the little boy. 'Thank you.'

They made up a bed in the spare room, and Joan took his clothes down to wash. They gave Roger an old nightshirt of Bob's to wear, and very small he looked in it, but he curled up tightly, looking for all the world as though he were trying to wrap a long tail around himself, and went to sleep at once.

'What are we going to do with him?' said Bob, squeezing the page-boy uniform through the mangle. 'He might be a wild boy. He might have been abandoned as a baby and brung up by wolves. Or rats. I read about a boy like that only last week in the paper.'

'Stuff and nonsense!'

'You don't know,' he insisted. 'He as good as told us. "I was a rat," he said. You heard him!'

'Rats don't have page-boy uniforms,' she said. 'Nor they don't speak, either.'

'He could have learned to speak by listening through the walls. And he could have found the uniform on a washing line,' Bob said. 'You depend on it, that's what happened. He's a wild boy, and he was brung up by rats. You can read about that kind of thing every week in the paper.'

'You're a silly old man,' said Joan.

THE PRIVY

Next morning Joan found the little boy lying in a heap of torn sheets and a terrible tangle of blankets and feathers, fast asleep.

She was going to cry out, because she feared that something had come in at the window and attacked him in the night; but he was sleeping so peacefully among all the destruction that she couldn't bring herself to wake him, though she was in despair over the damage.

'Come and look,' she said to old Bob, and he stood open-mouthed in the doorway.

'It looks like a hen-run after a fox has been in,' he said.

There wasn't a sheet or a blanket that hadn't been torn into strips. The pillow was burst open, and feathers lay like snow over the whole bed. Even

Bob's old nightshirt lay in tattered strips around the thin little body on the mattress.

'Oh, Roger,' said Joan. 'What have you done?'

The boy must have learned his name, because he woke up as soon as she said it, and sat up cheerfully.

'I'm hungry again,' he said.

'Look at what you've done!' she said. 'What were you thinking of?'

He looked around proudly.

'Yes, it was hard, but I done it,' he said. 'There's a lot more that needs chewing and tearing and I'll do that for you later.'

'You shouldn't tear things up!' she said. 'I've got to sew them all together again! We don't live like that, tearing things to pieces! Dear oh dear!'

The more she looked, the more damage she saw. It was going to take hours to repair.

Bob said, 'Did you do that because you was a rat?'

'Yes!' said Roger.

'Ah, well, that explains it,' the old man said, but Joan was in no mood to listen.

'That's got nothing to do with it! Never mind what he *was*, it's what he is *now* that matters! You shouldn't tear things up like this!' she cried, and she took his thin little shoulders and shook him, not hard, but enough to startle him.

'You come down the kitchen with me,' said Bob,

'and I'll tell you a thing or two. But first let's have some more manners. You've upset Joan, so you have to say sorry.'

'Sorry,' said the boy. 'I understand now. Sorry.'

'Come along,' said Bob, and took him by the hand. He could see Roger fidgeting, and guessed what he wanted to do, and took him to the privy just in time. 'Whenever you want to do that, you come in here,' he said.

'Yes, I will,' said the boy. 'That's a good idea.'

'Now come and have your breakfast. Wrap them pieces of nightshirt around you, you can't walk around naked, it ain't decent.'

Roger sat and watched Bob cut two slices of bread and prop them on the range to toast.

'I'll cook you an egg,' the old man said. 'You like eggs?'

'Oh, yes,' said Roger, 'thank you. I like eggs a lot.'

Bob cracked it into the frying pan, and Roger's jaw dropped as he saw the white spitting and bubbling and the golden yolk glistening in the middle.

'Ooh, that's pretty!' he said. 'I never seen the inside of an egg!'

'I thought you'd ate 'em before.'

'I ate 'em in the dark,' Roger explained.

'What, when you was a rat?'

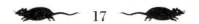

'Yes. Me and my brothers and sisters, we ate 'em in the dark, yes.'

'All right then,' said Bob peaceably, and slid the fried egg onto a plate, and buttered the toast.

Roger could barely hold himself back, but he remembered to say, 'Thank you,' before he put his face right down onto the plate and drew it back at once, gasping at the heat. His eyes brimming with tears, yellow yolk dripping off his mouth and nose, he turned to Bob in distress.

'Oh, I forgot you don't know how boys eat eggs,' the old man said. 'You probably thought you was a rat still, I expect.'

'Yes,' said Roger unsteadily, wiping at the mess with his fingers and licking them hard. 'I couldn't see the spoom, so I used me face.'

'It's a spoon, not a spoom. For eggs, you got to use a knife and fork. Here, do it like this, you copy me.'

Ignoring the tears and the egg on his face, Roger tried hard to do as Bob showed him. It was much harder to eat the egg with a fork than it had been to spoon up the bread and milk, but whenever he got discouraged, Bob told him to take a bite of toast. Roger held it up in both hands, and chewed it swiftly with his front teeth.

'I like toast,' he said. 'And egg.'

'Good. Now listen. We got to find out where you come from, and if there's someone who ought to be looking after you. Because you can't look after yourself, you're too little. And you can't stay here, because . . . Because you don't belong to us, see?'

'I want to stay here. I don't want to go anywhere.'

'Well, we got to do what's right. There's clever folk in the City Hall, they know what's right. We'll go along there by and by.'

'Yes, that's right,' said Roger.

THE CITY HALL

The office they needed was at the top of a grand staircase and along a panelled corridor. Bob and Joan had to hold the boy's hands, because he kept making little twitching movements as if he wanted to run away.

'D'you want the privy again? Is that it?' said Bob, and Joan hushed him for using a rude word in an important place, but he said, 'There's times when the privy is the most important place.'

'No,' said Roger, 'I just want to see what the wood on the walls tastes like.'

'He's an odd one, all right,' said Joan.

But she looked down at him fondly all the same, and he did look smart, with his brown hair brushed neatly and stuck down with water, and his uniform washed and pressed, and his vivid black eyes gazing around.

In the office where they deal with lost children, they had to sit down while a lady filled in a form. Bob was anxious to get things right.

'Properly speaking, we oughter gone to the Found Children Office, because this is a found child, only there ain't one as far as we could see,' he told her. 'So we come here instead.'

'You'd better tell me the details,' said the lady.

She took one of a dozen very sharp pencils out of a jar.

Roger watched her hand move to the jar, but he didn't watch it go back to the paper. As soon as he saw the pencils, he fell in love with them. His whole heart longed for them.

So while the lady and Bob and Joan leant across the desk talking, Roger's hand crept off his lap and slowly, carefully, over to the jar. He couldn't help it any more than a dog can help tiptoeing round the corner to eat the cat's food.

Bob was puzzled by what the lady was saying, which was why he was leaning over the desk to peer at the form she was filling in.

'No, no,' he said, 'that can't be right. He's got to come from somewhere. Someone must be missing him.'

'I can assure you,' she said, 'our records are very thorough. There are no lost children in the city. Not one, boy or girl.'

'But what about found children?'

'There's nothing we can do about found children. We deal with lost ones.'

'Gor,' said Bob, 'I'm baffled.'

'Have you asked him where he comes from?' the lady said.

And they all turned to Roger.

He looked up, pleased to be noticed, but a little guilty too. The stump of the pencil was just sticking out of his mouth, and he quickly sucked it inside and pressed his lips together; but the lead had marked his mouth, and there were little flecks of red paint all round it too.

Joan said, 'Child, what have you been doing?'

He tried to answer, but his mouth was full of pencil.

The lady said, 'That pencil was the property of the City Council! I shall have to ask you to pay for it!'

Bob paid up. It seemed a lot of money for a pencil. Roger could see he'd done something wrong, and as soon as he'd swallowed the last of it, he said, 'Sorry.'

'That's all very well, but you don't mean it, you bad boy,' said Joan, 'that's the trouble.'

The little boy was bewildered. Did he have to do something else as well as say sorry? What did *meaning it* mean? He looked from one grown-up to another, but they were all talking again.

'He must have said *something*,' the lady said. 'I'm trying to help you, though it's not my job to. I've shown you a lot of patience.'

Roger looked for the patience, but since he didn't know what they looked like, he supposed she meant the pencils.

'He said he was a rat,' Bob said. 'Not now, I mean he didn't say I *am* a rat, he said I *was* a rat. That's all he said.'

The lady looked at them all with distaste.

'I've got plenty to do without listening to nonsense,' she said.

'Well,' said Bob, 'all right. We won't trouble you any more.' And he got up, as massive as a hill beside the little boy. 'All I can say,' he went on, 'is that you ain't been much help. Good day to you.'

And with Roger between them, the old couple walked out of the City Hall.

'Ain't I going to stay there?' said the boy.

'No,' said old Bob.

'Is that because I'm a bad boy?'

'You ain't a bad boy.'

'But Joan said I was.'

'She was muddled,' said Bob, frowning. 'And now I'm muddled too.'

THE ORPHANAGE

Since it wasn't far away, they decided to go to the orphanage, just in case. But when they stood outside it, and looked at the broken windows and the cracked brickwork and the missing tiles on the roof, and smelt the orphanage smell drifting out of it (stale cigarette smoke, boiled cabbage, and unwashed bodies were the better parts), and heard someone crying steady sobs of misery through an upstairs window, Bob and Joan looked at each other and shook their heads.

They didn't need to speak. Holding Roger's hand, they turned and walked away.

The Police Station

There was a blue light outside the police station and a stout sergeant on duty at the desk. Roger looked at everything: the poster about Colorado beetles, the pictures of wanted criminals, the notices about bicycle safety. Since he couldn't read, he liked the picture of the Colorado beetle best. It looked very tasty.

'Well?' said the duty sergeant.

'We found this little boy last night,' said Bob. 'He don't know where he comes from. We thought we ought to bring him here.'

'I *do* know where I come from,' said Roger. 'I come from down under the market. There's a broken gutter behind the cheese stall and we had a nest in there. I was a rat,' he added, to make it clearer for the policeman.

The sergeant gave him a long cold look.

'Did you know there's such an offence as wasting police time?' he said.

'No, he's confused,' said Bob, anxious to explain. 'That's all it is. He probably had a bang on the head. He'd forgotten his name and all.'

'I knows it now though,' said the boy. 'I'm Roger.'

'Surname?' asked the sergeant.

'My surname . . .' said Roger, then worked it out. 'My surname is Sur Roger,' he declared, nodding firmly. 'That's who I am all right.'

'And we been to the City Hall,' Joan said, 'but they couldn't help, and—'

'And you're the only other place we could think of,' said Bob.

'If he's had a bang on the head,' said the sergeant, tapping a pencil on the desk, 'he ought be took to the hospital.'

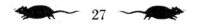

'Ah, we didn't think of that,' said Joan.

Roger was watching the sergeant's hand.

'That's a nice patient,' he said to him.

'Eh?'

'That patient you got. You been chewing the flat end. I like chewing the pointy end first.'

The sergeant gaped, and then recovered his wits.

'Did you notice that?' he said. 'When I said *hospital*, he said *patient*. That proves it. He's had a bang on the head. Either that or he's an escaped lunatic. But in any case he ought to be at the hospital. We can't take him here, we haven't got the facilities for lunatics, and in any case he ain't committed an offence. Yet,' he added, glaring down at Roger.

THE HOSPITAL

'No,' said the receptionist, 'he's not one of ours.'

They were very busy. People with broken legs or saucepans stuck on their heads sat waiting to be dealt with; doctors in white coats rushed about listening to heartbeats or taking temperatures; nurses emptied bedpans or bandaged cuts and grazes. It was the best place Roger had been in yet.

'But he might have had a bang on the head!' said Joan. 'Poor little boy, he thinks he was a rat!'

'H'mm,' said the receptionist, and wrote *rodent delusion* on a pink slip of paper.

'You got a lot of patients,' said Roger, looking with great interest at her desk.

'Got to be patient here,' she said, and passed the slip to the nearest doctor.

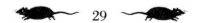

That puzzled Roger, but he soon forgot it. The doctor was an important-looking man with a smart black beard, and he said, 'Follow me.' So Bob and Joan took Roger into the consulting room, and watched anxiously as the doctor examined him.

First he felt all round Roger's head.

'No cranial contusions,' said the doctor.

Roger was fascinated by the rubber tube the doctor had round his neck, and when the doctor put the two hooks on the end into his own ears and placed the other end against Roger's chest, he could hardly hold himself back. His mouth was watering so much that he dribbled.

'Good appetite?' the doctor asked.

'Very good indeed,' said Joan. 'In fact—'

'Good,' said the doctor, twiddling Roger's knees.

Joan thought she'd better keep quiet.

The doctor examined Roger all over, and seemed to find only a healthy little boy.

'So what's this rodent delusion?' he said finally.

'Well, he says he was a rat,' said Bob. 'He's convinced of it.'

'A rat, were you?' said the doctor. 'When did you stop being a rat, then?'

'When I turned into a boy,' said Roger.

'Yes, I see. When was that?'

Roger twisted his lips. He looked at Bob for guidance, but the old man couldn't help, and neither could Joan.

'Dunno,' the boy said finally.

'And why did you stop being a rat?'

'Dunno.'

'Do you know what you are now?'

'I'm a boy.'

'That's right. And you're going to stay a boy, d'you hear?'

'Yes,' said Roger, nodding seriously.

'No more of this nonsense.'

'No.'

'Mustn't worry your . . .' the doctor hesitated. He'd been about to say 'your parents' but he looked at Bob and Joan again and said, 'Granny and Grandpa.'

Joan sat up a bit sharply. Roger looked puzzled. Bob took Joan's hand.

'He's no worry to us,' he said. 'As long as he's all right.'

'He's perfectly all right,' the doctor said. 'A normal healthy little boy.'

'But what should we do with him?' Joan said.

'Send him to school, of course,' said the doctor. 'Now I'm busy. Run along. Good day to you.'

The Daily Scourge

PALACE MAKE-OVER!

To celebrate the royal marriage, the palace is to be spectacularly redecorated.

OUT go fuddy-duddy antiques and dusty old pictures.

IN come designer furniture and a new, bright, up-to-the-minute look.

The redecoration is being carried out by attractive blonde, Sophie Trend-Butcher, 23, the brilliant young designer. The wallpaper is being hand-printed in gold.

While the work is being carried on in the palace, the royal family is staying at the Hotel Splendifico.

The old...

...and the cool

THE SCOURGE SAYS:

Yes, the redecoration is costing a fortune.

Yes, the money is coming from you and me.

BUT THIS IS OUR ROYAL FAMILY!

For Heaven's sake, where is our national pride?

We have the finest designers and craftspeople in the world – and here is a chance to show what they can really do.

And don't let's forget Prince Richard and his radiant bride-to-be.

Are they supposed to live in a museum?

Let's get behind the royal family in their attempt to bring the palace up to date!

SCHOOL

Since they hadn't had any luck, Bob and Joan took the little boy back home with them. He was perfectly content to trot along holding their hands, looking this way and that, for all the world as though he did belong to them.

'Granny and Grandpa,' said Joan scornfully.

'Well, that's not so bad,' said Bob. 'He might have thought *we* were rats, and all.'

'But what are we going to do with him?'

'Blowed if I know. But I don't want to spend another day trailing about and getting nowhere. I shall have to work late tonight, and I'm blooming tired.'

Roger didn't eat his bedclothes that night, though Joan thought the wooden bed-posts looked a little gnawed, and there was a damp splinter or two under his pillow the next morning.

'There's a good boy,' she said, cooking him some porridge on the range. 'You eat this and I'll take you down the school.'

Bob stayed at home to catch up with his cobbling. 'Listen carefully and do what the teacher says,' the old man told him. 'That's the way to learn.'

The school was a big building smelling of children. Roger liked it at once. There were boys and girls running about outside and throwing balls and fighting each other and shouting, and he thought this would be a fine place to spend a day.

'But you're not in fact his, er, any relation at all?' said the Head doubtfully to Joan as she stood holding Roger's hand in front of his desk.

'No. But we're looking after him for the time being, and the doctor said we had to bring him to school,' she said.

'I see,' said the Head. 'Well, Roger, how old are you?'

'Three weeks,' said Roger.

'Don't be silly now. That's not a good way to start. If you were only three weeks old you'd still be a baby. How old are you? Answer me properly this time.'

Roger shifted uneasily and looked up at Joan.

'He's not sure,' she said. 'I think he's lost his memory, poor lamb. He wouldn't know a thing like that.'

'He looks about nine,' said the Head. 'He can go in Mrs Cribbins's class. She won't stand any nonsense.'

A bell rang loudly and all the children stopped running and shouting and fighting and came inside. Roger was disappointed that the fun seemed to have stopped, but he sat where the teacher told him to, next to a boy with a runny nose.

'Now get out your pencils,' said Mrs Cribbins, 'and we'll have some arithmetic.'

Roger hadn't got a pencil, of course, or he'd have eaten it already. So he just watched as the other children took out theirs, and he knew he'd learned another word: *arithmetic* meant *snack*.

But to his absolute amazement the other children put the tasty ends of their pencils onto pieces of paper and drew lines with them. Roger had no idea you could do that, and he was so surprised and delighted that he laughed out loud.

'What's the joke?' snapped Mrs Cribbins. 'What's so funny? Eh?'

'They're making lines with their patients!' Roger said, eager to share his discovery.

'You're playing a dangerous game with *my* patience,' said Mrs Cribbins. 'Haven't you got a pencil?'

'No,' said Roger.

Mrs Cribbins couldn't believe that any pupil would come to school so badly prepared, and thought he was being cheeky.

'Go and stand in the corner,' she snapped.

Roger was happy to do that. He could smile at all the other children. But she made him face the wall, and that wasn't so interesting. And then the boy with the runny nose found a rubber band in his pocket and flicked it hard at Roger's neck.

Mrs Cribbins's back was turned, so naturally when Roger shouted and jumped and rubbed his neck she thought he was being naughty.

'I'm warning you,' she said, 'one more piece of nonsense and you're going to the Head.'

All the other children were enjoying it no end, and as soon as she turned away, someone else flicked another rubber band. Roger shouted again, and spun round to find Mrs Cribbins making for him with her hand raised.

Whether she would have smacked him or not no-one knew, because she didn't get any closer. Roger, seeing a threat, leapt up to bite her hand.

He got a good mouthful of it and shook hard, and Mrs

Cribbins shrieked and whacked him with her other hand, and the two of them struggled back and forth while the other children gasped with delight. Of course, the more she struggled, the more frightened Roger became and the tighter he bit, until at last she tugged her hand away. Roger, wild-eyed, was trembling and panting with his back to the wall, and no-one was laughing any more.

'Right,' said Mrs Cribbins, 'that's it for you, my lad.'

The door opened. There was the Head.

'What is all this noise?' he demanded.

'Look!' said Mrs Cribbins, holding up her hand. 'Look what this child has done! He's drawn blood! I'm bleeding!'

Actually she had to squeeze quite hard to force a drop of blood out, but it was real blood, sure enough.

The room was full of wide-open eyes, staring at the Head, at Mrs Cribbins, at Roger.

The Head seemed to get bigger and bigger, and Roger to get smaller and smaller.

'Come with me,' said the Head in a dangerous voice.

All the children knew that voice. It was the voice that meant he was going to use the cane. He didn't use it very often but the occasions when he did were terrifying. There would be a deep silence over the whole school, and a sick feeling in everyone's stomach, and no-one would dare to look at the victim before he went into the dreadful place where he'd be beaten, or to speak to him after he came out, sniffling and limping. And everyone would be quiet and unhappy for a day or so afterwards.

And now Roger was going to be caned, and everyone knew it but him.

He thought the Head was taking him away from the cruel woman who'd frightened him, so he smiled up at him and said, 'You can make lines on paper with them things. I thought they was called patients at first but they got other names too. I never knew you could make lines with 'em.'

All the children sat open-mouthed. How could this new boy dare to speak to the Head in this familiar friendly way? It was the cheekiest thing they'd ever heard. Some of them felt shocked, and some felt gleeful at the thought of the extra punishment he'd surely get, and some felt admiration.

'This way,' said the Head.

Roger followed.

Silence fell over the classroom. Mrs Cribbins ran some water over her hand and dried it on her handkerchief and took a plaster from her handbag and carefully placed it over the bite, and the children watched her solemnly without making a sound.

Then, just as she was opening her mouth to tell them to turn back to their work, there came a wild scream from down the corridor.

No-one had ever heard a scream like that. When a boy went to be caned, he tried as hard as he could to make no noise at all, and some of the toughest ones managed to stop themselves even from whimpering, and were greatly admired for it. But not even the most babyish victim would have screamed as long and as wildly as Roger was screaming. The sound seemed to drill into everyone's head and scrape round and round in their skulls. Some of them put their hands over their ears.

Those who didn't block off the sound soon heard other sounds too: the Head's voice raised in anger, furniture crashing, doors banging, footsteps running down the corridor – it was the most exciting arithmetic lesson they'd ever had.

'Look, he's running away!' shouted a girl, and pointed out at the schoolyard.

Roger was racing for the gate, with the Head in red-faced pursuit. All the children crowded to the window to watch, ignoring Mrs Cribbins's efforts to make them sit down. They jumped and clapped and laughed with shocked delight as Roger fought and screamed and bit and kicked and finally tore himself free, leaving the Head flailing at the empty air behind him.

Then Roger scrambled up and over the gate in a second or so, and vanished round the corner.

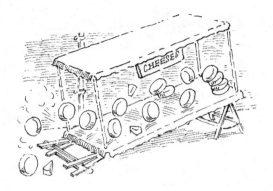

No Escape

Roger ran in terror through the streets and
alleys till he came to the market-place,
where he ran up and down between the
stalls, looking this way and that, and gulping and
shaking with sobs. His face was wet and his nose
was running and he looked a thorough mess.

Finally he got down on all fours and crawled
under the cheese stall and made for the drainpipe
in the corner; but that was a bad mistake. He wasn't
quite as small as he thought he was, and before he
knew what was happening, he'd knocked away one

of the trestles holding the stall up.

At once the whole top fell down. Cheeses rolled, slid, flopped and bounced in all directions. Somehow, every dog in the area suddenly learned that there was free cheese in the market-place, and within seconds a yapping, barking mob was making for the overturned stall. Roger was terrified of dogs, and when he saw them coming he screamed and cowered in the corner, where it was easy to catch him.

And five minutes later Roger was in the police station again.

'Who's that?' said the sergeant, as the constable came back to report his arrest. 'Little boy in a page's uniform? Let me look at him.'

Roger was crouching in the corner when the sergeant opened the cell door, and as soon as he saw daylight he tried to dart out, but the sergeant grabbed him.

'Ah, I thought it was you,' he said. 'Born trouble-maker, you are. As soon as I heard the words "market" and "cheese", I remembered you, just like that. Good thing I made a record of your address. See how your old auntie and uncle feel about coming down here to bail you out.'

When Bob arrived, he wasn't pleased at all.

'Well, Sergeant?' he said, across the counter.

'What's the boy done? Last thing I knew, he was at school.'

'Ah,' said the sergeant triumphantly, 'well he ain't any more. And he's in real trouble, your lad. Mayhem and criminal damage. I shouldn't wonder if it amounted to riot. Bring him out, Constable.'

'Riot? How can one little boy have a riot all on his own?'

The constable came out with Roger firmly in his grip. As soon as the boy saw Bob, he smiled up with happy relief.

'Ah, I was worried,' he said. 'It was all because I started to worry. But I wouldn't have got worried if the Head hadn't hit me.'

'He hit you?' said Bob. 'Why?'

'I don't know. It's mysterious,' said Roger. 'She just called him a Head, but he wasn't only a head. I thought he was just a head, on a table maybe, or he might have had a little stand, and I wanted to see it work. But he had arms and legs and everything. And I didn't know what he was going to do. He made me bend over and I thought he was going to play leapfrog like I seen 'em in the playground, only suddenly whoosh! He hit my tail with a blooming stick! Ooh, that hurt awful. I wished he *was* a head with no arms and legs, then he wouldn't be able to hurt boys like that. So I ran away and I got in a muddle with the cheese. Then they caught me and put me in that room in there. Can we go now?'

'Sergeant, this ain't a desperate criminal,' said Bob. 'This is a little boy who don't know what's what. You ain't going to use the whole majesty of the law to punish a little boy for a bit of mischief, are you?'

'What about the damage to my stall?' demanded the cheesemonger, who had just arrived. 'And all my cheeses! Who's going to pay for them?'

Bob's heart sank. 'I suppose I'll have to pay for the damage,' he said. 'Make up the account and send it to me. I'm not a rich man, mind.'

'Sergeant,' said the constable, 'ain't this the boy who had some tale about being a rat?'

'Yes,' said Roger eagerly. 'I had a tail all right. It was a good 'un.'

'Be quiet,' said the sergeant sternly. 'Rats don't belong in decent society. They ought to be exterminated.'

Roger didn't know what exterminated meant, of course, but he didn't like the sound of it. He clung tight to Bob and said nothing.

They agreed that Bob would pay for the cheese, and that Roger would behave himself in future.

'And if I see you back here,' the sergeant said, 'you'll be in terrible trouble. Don't you forget it.'

The Daily Scourge

SIX OF THE BEST

Six MPs are standing out against the proposal to ban the cane in schools.

'It made me the man I am!' claimed Sir Bernard Brute, MP. 'Children today are getting out of control. They must be beaten hard and often.'

Sir Bernard Brute, MP, demonstrating the strength of his convictions

Some teachers claim that the cane has no place in the caring and compassionate society they want to bring about.

'It is a relic of the Middle Ages,' said a teacher yesterday.

'We no longer need to rely on torture to encourage good behaviour.'

But other teachers disagree.

'There is a hard core of violent hooligans in our schools,' said Mr George Hackett, Head of St Lawrence's Primary School. 'If we take away the cane, we will leave teachers without the power to defend themselves.'

THE SCOURGE SAYS:

KEEP ON WHACKING!

These feeble so-called 'experts' who say that the cane is cruel are helping no-one.

A quick smack never did any child any harm.

And in today's schools there are some little brutes and bullies who could do with a taste of the cane to keep them in order.

Support the six of the best!

Vote in our readers' poll on *page 10.*

A Curious And Interesting Case

It was a fine sunny morning, and the Philosopher Royal was taking a nap.

Normally at this time of day the King liked to chat with the Philosopher Royal over a cup of coffee and a biscuit, discussing things like why toast always fell on the buttered side or whether flies looped the loop before landing on the ceiling, but with the royal family away at the Hotel Splendifico while the palace was being decorated ready for the royal wedding, there was little call for philosophy.

The servant who woke the Philosopher Royal up for lunch was a cousin of the constable who'd arrested Roger, and he told him all about it, knowing the old man's curious turn of mind.

'Said he was a rat?'

'Said he *used* to be a rat, sir. He was ever so sure

about it. My cousin said it give him a creepy feeling all up his spine. He don't like rats.'

The Philosopher Royal made a note of the policeman's name, and after lunch he went to the police station to ask about the case. The sergeant was very impressed to see his card.

'Now when I see the word "Philosopher" in connection with the word "Royal",' he said, 'I wonder whether I'm right in guessing that you might have met the Prince's fiancée. What's she like? Is she as pretty as she looks in her pictures?'

The Philosopher Royal told him. 'But this boy who said he was a rat,' he went on. 'Have you got his address?'

'Not *was*,' said the sergeant. 'He said he used to be, but he wasn't any more. Oh, yes, it's all on file.' The sergeant read out Bob and Joan's address. 'But you be warned by me,' he said, 'that boy's a bad influence, rat or no rat. He'll come to a bad end.'

'I am most grateful,' said the Philosopher Royal. 'Good day to you.'

In the cobbler's shop Bob was waxing some thread. 'Morning, sir,' he said. 'What can I do for you?'

'You are Mr Bob Jones? Guardian of a boy called Roger?'

Bob looked alarmed. Then he looked careful.

'What's he done now?' he said.

'I would like to see him. Is he at home?'

'He's in the laundry room, helping my wife. You got to keep an eye on him, else he eats the soap. But who might you be, sir?'

'My interest is purely philosophical. May I see the boy?'

'Well, I don't see why not. Step this way, sir . . .'

Bob led the Philosopher Royal into the laundry room, which was full of warm steamy air. Joan was stirring some sheets in hot water with a big stick, and Roger was feeding a pillowcase into the mangle and squeezing the water out, tasting it from time to time.

'Mrs Jones?' said the Philosopher Royal. 'And Roger?'

Joan dried her hands and gathered Roger close to her. He peered up at the Philosopher Royal with his bright black eyes wide.

'Did you want some washing done, sir?' said Joan.

'No, no. My washing is done by the palace laundrymaids. I was hoping for a brief talk with your, er, with the young, with Roger.'

'He's not in trouble, is he, sir?' she said anxiously.

'No, no,' said the Philosopher Royal, 'this is a purely philosophical investigation.'

'Well, I suppose you could talk in the parlour if

you liked . . .' she said, and led them through to a
little room that smelled of furniture polish. 'I'll
leave you to get on with it,' she said, 'because I've
got a lot of washing to get through. Now, Roger, you
be a good boy, and answer the gentleman politely.
No nibbling.'

When Joan had left, the Philosopher Royal sat
down and looked at Roger: a little boy of eight or
nine, perhaps, dressed in a uniform.

'Now, Roger,' he began, 'why are you wearing a
page-boy's uniform?'

'I dunno. I expect I forgot, but I'm not sure. If I
could remember whether I'd forgot it I'd know if I
had, but I probably forgot without remembering it.'

The Philosopher Royal was used to problems of

epistemology, so he made sense of that with no trouble at all.

'I see,' he said. 'Now, would you let me examine you properly? It won't hurt,' he added.

'I expect so,' said Roger.

The Philosopher Royal was thinking of the book he'd write about this. What a discovery! There'd been children brought up by wolves before, but no-one had ever studied a child brought up by rats. It would make him famous! Rubbing his hands together, the Philosopher Royal left Roger chewing one of the tassels off the lampshade and went to speak to Bob.

'You want to take him away?' said Bob, frowning.

'Just to make some tests, you know – weigh him, measure him, that sort of thing. To see how a human child is affected by being among rats. It's a question of exceptional philosophical importance.'

'But when he was among the rats he weren't a human child,' said Bob. 'He's a human child *now*.'

'Well, of course, he wasn't really a rat,' said the Philosopher Royal, thinking how simple these people were.

'H'mm,' said Bob. 'You bring him back here this evening, and don't you hurt him. I don't know what legal responsibility we got, but he come to us and knocked, and that's enough for me. And he's a lovely little feller, for all his chewing. You look after him proper.'

'No question about that,' said the Philosopher Royal.

Roger had finished off all the tassels except one. Bob sighed and snapped off the last one and dropped it into the little boy's hand.

'I dunno how you digest some of this, I really don't,' he said.

'No,' said Roger. 'It's a mystery to me.'

'Now you go along with this gentleman and do as he says, all right? And he'll bring you back home in time for supper.'

Roger bowed good-bye to Bob and went out happily with the Philosopher Royal.

A PHILOSOPHICAL INVESTIGATION

On the way up the palace staircase, Roger said, 'I been here before.'

'Are you sure, my boy?' said the Philosopher Royal.

'Oh, yes. I slid down them banisters.'

The Philosopher Royal thought: *Cannot distinguish truth from fantasy.*

Once in his study the first thing he did was to weigh Roger, and then he measured him, and then he listened to his heart, and then he counted his teeth. He didn't learn much, but he did notice that Roger had perfectly human teeth, not a bit like a rat's. There was no point in looking for a tail: the boy was human all the way down, no doubt about it.

'Now then, Roger,' said the Philosopher Royal, 'let's do some mental tests. What is two and three?'

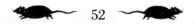

'Two and three what?' said Roger, very puzzled.

'Well, if you have two things, and you add three more, how many have you got?'

'Ah, that depends. If they're really little things you still wouldn't have very much, but if they're big things you couldn't even carry 'em,' Roger explained.

'Yes, I see. What's half of four?'

'Cheese,' said Roger. 'Cheddar. Quarter of four's Cheddar too. Quarter of five'd be Stilton. One is Lancashire, two is Wensleydale—'

'I don't understand,' said the Philosopher Royal, writing everything down.

'Well, they come to the stall and they ask for a half pound of number four, and that's Cheddar, or a quarter pound of number five, and that's Stilton. I likes that one. You get worms in it. Only sometimes they say just half instead of half a pound, that's how I knew what you meant. You got to keep your wits about you,' he told the Philosopher Royal.

'Oh, indeed. Now tell me, when did you learn to speak?'

'When I changed into a boy.'

'Yes, but you didn't really *change*, did you? You were a boy all the time. Perhaps you *thought* you were a rat. But rats can't—'

'I never thought at all when I was a rat! I just was! So I never thought I was a rat. I never started thinking till I was a boy. Now I think I'm a boy. But it's making me confused. I hope I don't get irritated.'

'All right,' said the Philosopher Royal nervously. He wasn't used to dealing with children, after all, and he might have expected them to be irrational. But even the King was more rational than this child. 'Don't get upset,' he went on. 'Now I'm just going to ask you some questions about the world we live in. Do you know the name of the Prime Minister?'

Roger laughed as if the Philosopher Royal had made a joke.

'No!' he said happily.

'And the name of this city?'

'I never knew it had a name. I thought it just was, like a rat.'

'What is the name of the King?'

'Ah, I know that,' said Roger. 'He's called King Henry.'

'And the Queen?'

'No. She's not Henry. She's Queen Margaret.'

'And the Prince?'

'No, he's not Henry nor Margaret. He's Richard.'

'Good. You know all their names. Well done.'

'And I know the name of who the Prince is going to marry. She's called Mary Jane.'

'Mary Jane?' said the Philosopher Royal. 'No, no. She's called Aurelia.'

Roger looked doubtful. 'She might be called Aurelia as well,' he admitted, 'but in the kitchen they calls her Mary Jane. I do know that.'

The Philosopher Royal wrote down: *Fantasy-identification with figures of glamour. Common among lower classes. Indicates humble origin for boy.*

'What's that mean,' said Roger, 'what you just wrote?'

'I'm making notes,' said the Philosopher Royal. 'To remind me of our conversation.'

'Ah,' said Roger. 'You're probably a bit forgetful, then. Once you've learned to remember things you won't need to do that. You can keep 'em all folded up in your head. They don't take up much room,' he went on. 'As long as you fold 'em flat. I seen Joan do that with the sheets, and I thought, there's a good idea. So now I folds and irons all the things in my head and I stack 'em neat. I know where they all are.'

'Remarkable,' said the Philosopher Royal, and wrote: *Insane. Sensory-intellectual delusions, paranoid in nature.*

Roger was eyeing the bell pull in the corner.

'Excuse me,' he said, 'but you know that rope? Well, there's a loose bit of thread at the bottom. That could be dangerous, someone could trip over that and hurt theirselves. So maybe I ought to chew it off, just that little bit of thread. If it would help,' he added.

'Well . . .' said the Philosopher Royal, and then, 'Yes. Why not?'

He turned a page and wrote: *Gross and unnatural appetite.*

Roger nibbled off the bit of thread, which was almost as long as his fingernail, and then found that he'd accidentally pulled loose a longer piece, so he had to chew that too; and that brought with it a very tasty knot, flavoured with a length of gold thread from the tassel, and before a minute had gone by Roger was blissfully eating his way up the bell pull itself.

Seeing him eating so well, the Philosopher Royal turned his mind to thoughts of food and nourishment, and what rats eat, and then by a logical process to the question of what eats rats.

'Aha!' he said. 'Wait here, my boy. Don't go away.'

And he left the study and hurried to his sitting room, where he scooped up his cat Bluebottle and hurried back. Bluebottle was not a philosophical cat; she was lazy and greedy and exceptionally stupid. She had no objection to being picked up and carried somewhere else, because there was very little in her head to object with. So, tucked under the Philosopher Royal's arm, she just dangled her back legs and stuck out her front ones and half-opened her eyes . . .

Until they went into the study.

As soon as Roger saw the cat, he shrieked and leapt away. The window was open, and he dived out and into a flower bed and then scrambled to his feet and ran, and Bluebottle chased after him, automatically.

But she was a lazy cat, and when she saw she'd have to run further than the edge of the lawn she slowed down and gave up. She forgot about him almost at once and sat down to groom herself, while the Philosopher Royal stared out of the window, amazed, and Roger vanished out of the palace gates.

MR TAPSCREW

In the market that day there happened to be a man from a fair. The fair was in the next town at the time, and it moved around, as fairs do, but this man had come to Roger's town because he'd heard a rumour that he wanted to investigate. He was the proprietor of one of the shows in the fair, and his name was Oliver Tapscrew.

Early that evening, Mr Tapscrew was standing at the bar of the Black Horse, a pint of bitter in his hand and a fat cigar in his mouth, talking to the owner of the jellied-eel stall from the market.

'I heard tell of something odd recently,' said Mr Tapscrew. 'I dunno if I heard it right – something about a boy who was really a rat. You ever heard of anything like that?'

'Rats?' said the jellied-eel man. 'No. Used to be a

plague of 'em. But the Mayor and Corporation got a first-class firm of exterminators in. They exterminated everything in sight: rats, mice, cockroaches, fleas, lice, you name it. Wiped 'em out. Clean as a whistle. Place is so clean now I don't even have to wipe my stall down. Thanks, I'll have another.'

Mr Tapscrew reminded himself not to eat any jellied eels while he was here.

'They ain't really been exterminated,' said a horse-dealer. 'Rats and mice. You couldn't. They're cunning, they are, they got cunning blood. They take samples of the poison and they learn how to digest it. I shouldn't wonder if there's a race of super-rats down the sewers. With fangs like *that*. And a hatred for the whole human race. The rats' time is coming, you mark my words.'

Mr Tapscrew listened, and bought more pints of beer, and noticed with satisfaction that although nobody *knew* anything about rats, or boys who'd been rats, they all enjoyed a good shiver when they thought about them. Good shivers were good business.

He sipped his beer, while his fertile brain played with the notion of rats: super-rats, rat-boys, a whole freak-show of rat-humans, owned and trained and exhibited by Oliver Tapscrew – no, Professor Tapscrew – that would look good on the sign. He'd have it painted as soon as he got back.

Then he felt a hand on his arm, and turned to see a small greengrocer with a dapper little moustache.

'Excuse me,' said the greengrocer, 'that rat-boy you was talking about – I just seen him.'

'My dear fellow!' said Mr Tapscrew. 'D'you know him, then? Where is he?'

'If he's who I think he is,' said the small man, 'he's been took in by neighbours of mine. You wouldn't think he was a rat, really, he looks just like a boy. But he's got an unnatural appetite. There's something uncanny about it, mark my words.'

'Did you say you'd seen him?' said Mr Tapscrew.

'Yes. Just going down that alley over there, looking furtive.'

'Thanks,' said Mr Tapscrew. 'Have a drink, old man!'

He thrust some money into the greengrocer's hand, and hurried off down the alley.

It was a grubby little place between the municipal workhouse and the Hotel Salmagundi. At first Mr Tapscrew couldn't see a living creature there, but hearing a soft clatter, he stopped to look behind a mound of empty cardboard boxes, wine bottles, and soggy vegetable crates.

There he saw a small boy, crouching by a tipped-over dustbin, scooping something creamy out of a carton. He looked up, and Mr Tapscrew noted with pleasure the boy's quick-moving jaws, the appalling stink from the dustbin, and the bright black eyes that looked back at him.

'Tell me,' said Mr Tapscrew, 'I wonder if by any chance you might happen to be the boy who used to be a rat?'

'Yes,' said Roger. 'Only now I'm—'

'Good! Excellent!'

'I didn't mean to knock the dustbin over, only I—'

'Don't worry about it, dear boy. Come with me!'

Reluctantly abandoning the last of the smoked salmon mousse that had been in the dustbin for six days, Roger took Mr Tapscrew's hand and walked away with him, because he thought he ought to be a good boy.

WHERE'S HE GONE?

When Roger didn't come back, Bob and Joan weren't sure when they should start to worry. On the one hand he was with the Philosopher Royal, who was sure to be looking after him properly, but on the other hand the man had said he'd bring Roger back, and he hadn't.

And on the third hand there was the fact that Bob and Joan had never had a child to look after before, and didn't know what to expect or whether they ought to worry. And on the fourth hand there was the fact that they were worrying about him already, because they were very fond of him, strange as he was.

It was a good thing they only had four hands between them, or they'd have been even more worried. Joan even snapped at Bob, a thing she hardly ever did.

'What are you wasting your time with them silly slippers for?' she said. 'No-one's got feet that small, and what that leather must have cost I can't imagine.'

Bob was putting the last stitches in the scarlet slippers he'd been making. He looked up over his glasses and said, 'If a cobbler can't do something for the pure craftsmanship of it, it's a poor thing. They'll come in useful one day, don't you fret.'

He wasn't cross; he knew she was worried. When the old cuckoo clock struck nine, Bob put the slippers away and took off his glasses.

'Well, that's late enough,' he said. 'I'm not going to wait any more. I'm going down the palace to see what that man's been up to.'

'I'll come with you,' said Joan. 'I can't bear sitting waiting.'

'Funny, innit,' said Bob, 'we been sitting by this fire for thirty-two years, but it never seemed like waiting before.'

They put on their hats and coats and went to the tradesmen's entrance of the palace. Some soldiers were playing football in the courtyard, and another was smoking and reading the paper in a sentry box, and took no notice. Bob and Joan could hear giggling from somewhere inside, and the sound of glasses clinking.

'Yeah?' said the maid who opened the door, and hiccuped. 'Oops!'

'We come for the little boy,' said Bob firmly. 'It's his bedtime. The gentleman who wanted to investigate him must be finished by now.'

The maid vanished, shutting them outside. After a few minutes, during which Bob and Joan had to blow on their hands and stamp up and down to keep warm, she came back.

'Dr Prosser says he ran home,' she said, and was about to close the door when Bob put his foot in it.

'No he didn't,' said Bob. 'I want a word with Dr Prosser.'

The maid reluctantly opened the door. There was a party going on in the servants' hall, and she hurried them past and along to the door of the Philosopher Royal's apartment.

'Oh dear, oh dear,' said the Philosopher Royal when he opened the door.

'Where's our Roger?' said Joan.

'He ran away. Couldn't concentrate. Just leapt out of the window and ran home.'

'Ah, but he didn't,' said Bob. 'He never turned up.'

'And what did you do to him?' said Joan.

'A number of tests. They showed quite clearly

that the boy is deranged. A psychotic personality disorder, with paranoid delusions combined with fantasy-identification with figures of glamour. Marked retardation of intellectual development. In short, he has a hopeless future, though he might find a useful occupation in some humble manual activity.'

'Never mind that,' said Bob, who was getting hot and bothered. 'We didn't send him to you to be tested because we wanted it. *You* wanted it. You come and took him, and now you've lost him, and we want him back. What are you going to do about it?'

'Ah,' said the Philosopher Royal cleverly, smiling and shaking his head, 'no, no, no. I think you're making an elementary error about the nature of language. When you say, "You've lost him," that seems to imply the notion of fault, of blame, of the whole discredited apparatus of causality. We don't talk in those terms any more. As a matter of fact, meaning itself is a problematic concept when nothing is final and everything is a matter of interpretation into terms which themselves—'

'I don't understand a word of that,' said Bob, 'but I tell you what, it makes me feel sick. You lost that little boy, and there's an end of it. When did he go? You can say that, I suppose?'

The Philosopher Royal gulped.

'About three o'clock,' he said.

Bob turned and walked away, but Joan hadn't finished.

'Someone oughter smacked you when you still did believe in things,' she said. 'It's too late now, else I'd do it myself.'

And she took Bob's arm and they went down the silent stairs, past the laughter in the servants' hall, past the soldiers playing football in the moonlight, and out of the palace grounds.

'Where to now?' said Bob, as they looked down over the chilly rooftops in the frosty air.

'Don't know,' she said. 'We ain't just going to give up though, are we, Bob?'

'You're a silly old woman,' he said. 'We'll find him, never mind how long it takes. We just need a clue, that's all. But I'm blessed if I know where to start.'

You Want 'Em Nauseated

'That's it! *Professor Tapscrew's Amazing Rat-Boy! The Wonder of the Age! See this sub-human monster wallow in abominable filth!* That's it, paint him as ferocious as you can. You got all those words written down? Get on with it, then,' said Mr Tapscrew, slapping the sign-painter on the back. 'Now, Martha, how's that costume coming on? Let's have a look at that tail. Dear dear dear, that's not nearly scabby enough. Make it six foot long and all covered with pustules. We could bung a few pustules on his face, come to think of it. Oh, and whiskers.'

In Mr Tapscrew's caravan, Roger sat peaceably chewing a leather belt and watching all this activity. These people didn't mind him eating anything.

'Here! Ron! Make that cage a bit smaller. We can

get more punters in the tent then, and the rat-boy'll look all the bigger. Rig up a sort of sewer-looking thing – big round pipe kind of effect for him to squat in – yeah, like that. Do they have nests? Do rats have nests? Here, you,' he said, nudging Roger with his foot, 'do rats have nests?'

'Yeah,' said Roger. These questions were much easier than the philosophical ones. 'Nice and cosy,' he added.

'You heard him,' said Mr Tapscrew. 'Get some rotten old bones off the lion-tamer and bung 'em in. Now – lights. We want to go for a sort of ghastly look. We want him to sort of emerge from the shadows. A pool of light near the punters, so he can come up front and do a bit of snarling when it gets quiet. Here,' he went on, struck by a sudden thought, 'd'you think he ought to have a name?'

'I got a name,' said Roger. 'It's new, I ain't hardly used it. It's Roger.'

'No, no, no. A wild sort of name. Like . . . Rorano, the Rat-Boy. What d'you think?'

'That's daft,' said his wife Martha, sewing on a pustule. 'If he's got a name, they'll only sympathize. You don't want that. You want 'em nauseated.'

'You know,' said Mr Tapscrew with admiration, 'that's why I married you. What a brain! Rat-Boy he is, then.'

'And he mustn't speak, neither,' she said. 'Just snarl and grunt. Here, you, Rat-Boy, come here and try this on.'

Since Roger hadn't been listening, he didn't know who she meant, and went on chewing his belt.

'Give him a clout, Ollie,' she said. 'He's got to learn.'

Mr Tapscrew bent very close and said, 'Now you listen careful, else you'll be sorry. You ain't Roger any more. You're Rat-Boy, understand? Don't forget it. Now try this costume on.'

Roger was puzzled, but he did as he was told. It 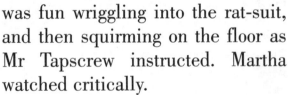 was fun wriggling into the rat-suit, and then squirming on the floor as Mr Tapscrew instructed. Martha watched critically.

'It's a bit on the loose side,' she said. 'I'll have to take it in. And he ought to swing that tail around. Here, Rat-Boy, swing your back-side, get that tail swishing.'

Roger tried, but it just trailed limply on the floor. She shook her head.

'He'll have to practise,' she said. 'Can't go in front of the public like that. He looks too tame altogether. We'll have to do something about that.'

The Daily Scourge

TRUTH

THE WEDDING OF THE YEAR!

His Royal Highness Prince Richard and the Lady Aurelia were married yesterday in the magnificent surroundings of the cathedral.

The bride was radiant in her white lace and satin wedding dress.

'She looks like a fairy princess!' was the verdict of the crowd, who had stood all night long to see the ceremony.

As the coach rolled back bearing the Prince and Princess, thousands of happy well-wishers waved flags and cheered.

Their eternal love sealed with a kiss

one's hearts by turning to her Prince and giving him a long kiss.

'You can tell they're really in love,' said Dorothy Plunkett, the *Scourge*'s royal expert. 'It's the real thing this time for the playboy Prince.'

A KISS ON THE BALCONY

Outside the Palace, the crowd had something else to cheer about when the royal couple appeared on the balcony to wave to their loyal subjects.

Princess Aurelia won every

GETTING MARRIED?

WIN . . .

- A replica of the royal wedding dress
- A fortnight's honeymoon at the Hotel Splendifico
- A right royal make-over for your dream house!
See page 5

A LOAD OF OLD COD

B ob and Joan decided that after their experiences with the police, they'd be better off not going to them again, and they weren't very impressed with the other officials they'd spoken to on Roger's account, either. As they wandered home through the market square they felt sorely puzzled.

'You don't think he's run right away, do you?' said Joan. 'I think he was feeling that we were his home. I *think* he was.'

Just then the door of the Black Horse opened, and out came their neighbour Charlie, the dapper little greengrocer, staggering slightly.

'Evening, Bob,' he said. 'Hello, Joan. Here – you know that little boy . . . Where's that sleeve gone?' He was having trouble with his coat.

'Go on,' said Joan at once, helping him into the sleeve, 'what about a little boy?'

'Aha,' said Charlie. 'I'm getting to that. Lot of talk about rats in the pub today. There was a flash-looking feller with a big cigar asking about 'em. Seems there's a monster about,' he added, stepping alongside very carefully, as if he wasn't sure the ground was there.

'Get away,' said Bob. 'What sort of a monster?'

'Half child,' said Charlie solemnly, 'and half rat.'

Joan's hand tightened on Bob's arm. Charlie was having trouble finding the end of his scarf, because it was inside his coat at the back. Bob pulled it out for him.

'Thank you,' he said, bowing to him and staggering a little.

'Well, what about the little boy?' Joan said.

'Ah,' said Charlie, trying to lay a finger alongside his nose and nearly poking his eye out. 'Coming to that. This man Stewtap – Plumbscrew – summing – he was looking for this rat-monster because he was going to put him on show, Eric reckoned. Eric seen the man before, in a fair, exhibiting a mermaid in a tank. And Eric – he paid his money and went in to see the mermaid, and you know what he says? He says – ooh Lor, listen to this – he says the top half was prime, but the bottom half was a load of old cod! Lor! What d'you think of that, eh?'

He was nearly doubled up, choking with laughter.

'On account of her tail,' he wheezed. 'A load of old cod!'

'Very funny,' said Bob, 'yeah, that's a good 'un. What was the feller called again?'

'And what about the little boy?' said Joan, stamping her foot. 'I swear, Charlie Hoskins, you're driving me mad. *What about the little boy?*'

'I seen him,' said Charlie, 'and I told the man about him.'

'What? Where? When?'

'This afternoon. Down the alley. Wossisname again – Tapstew – Thumbscrap – can't remember – he was looking for him, and I showed him where he'd gone. Ooh, I feel ill. Ooh, I feel awful . . .'

'Well, there's one consolation,' said Joan. 'You'll feel worse in the morning.'

'Oh, good . . . oh, Lor . . . Here,' said Charlie, clinging to Bob's sleeve, 'I'll get his name in a minute. Tap – Snap – Screwfish – 's no good, 's gone. Goo'night.'

'Well,' said Bob to Joan once they'd helped Charlie inside his front door and seen it safely shut, 'I suppose that's a start.'

THE WONDER OF THE AGE

Two days later, and many miles down the road, St Matthew's Fair opened for business. It was always the same fair, but in this town it opened on St Matthew's Day, so it was St Matthew's Fair; in that town it opened over Michaelmas, so it was the Michaelmas Fair; and it reached another town on May Day, so it was the May Fair. The stall-owners and merry-go-round proprietors, and the man who ran the ghost train, and the owner of the Death-Defying Wall of Doom all knew what time of year it was by what town they happened to be in.

They arrived late at night and by the light of many lamps and lanterns they set up their stalls and assembled their roundabouts and bolted together their rides in the cattle market, under the old town castle.

Mr Tapscrew was putting the final touches to his stall as the sun rose over the market cross.

'No,' he said, 'we still need a bit more filth and squalor. It looks almost respectable in there. We need mud and rotten vegetables. We need dung, really, but there's a limit to what the public will stand, more's the pity. A good show ought to be a little ahead of the public, but not too far, and I think they'd draw the line at dung.'

'So would I,' said his wife. 'We've got to live with him, remember. Here — what about charging 'em extra to feed him? We'll have a feeding time, every hour on the hour, special price. And the beauty of it is,' she went on, 'we don't have to supply the food! They bring it theirselves!'

He looked at her fondly. 'Genius,' he murmured.

'Rig up a sign,' she said. 'Make it fancy, with all toothsome words. You're good at that.'

Less than an hour later, everything was ready.

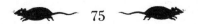

THE WONDER OF THE AGE!

Professor Tapscrew presents

The World's only genuine living

!! RAT-BOY !!

This half-human, half-rodent altogether ABOMINABLE creature *discovered living in the Filth of the Sewers* will demonstrate his

Loathsome and Unnatural Appetite

by Eating Anything

put before him by the Public.

Feeding Time: every Hour on the Hour.

WARNING:

The Rat-boy's Savage and Ferocious Instincts make him

DANGEROUS TO APPROACH.

Wonder! Marvel! Shudder!

'Smashing,' said Mrs Tapscrew.

The first visitors came soon afterwards. Seven people, grown-ups and children, crowded into the little booth and stared down into a pit lined with crumbling plaster and rotten planks. The floor was covered in dirty straw, cabbage-stumps, and bits of vegetable too decayed to recognize.

'Eurgghh,' said a girl.

'Look!' said a boy. 'He's coming out! Yuk!'

As the little boy pointed, something stirred at the back of the pit, and first there appeared a hand, then skinny arms, then a face—

'Eeeuuurrgghh! Yuchh! Eurghhhh!'

Roger had been thoroughly decorated with scabs and pustules and a couple of great red boils for good measure. His rat-suit had been taken in to fit him tightly, and as he scrambled out he swung his horrible leathery tail in the way he'd practised.

Cries of revulsion and disgust greeted him. He was delighted. He smiled up happily, showing the blacked-out teeth Mrs Tapscrew had painted.

'Here, Rat-Boy! Eat this!' someone called, and threw in a rotten potato.

Roger hadn't eaten anything that day. The Tapscrews had kept him hungry on purpose, and although he'd chewed a bit of wood and swallowed some straw, there was no nourishment in that; so he

seized the potato at once, and remembering what Bob and Joan had told him, said, 'Thank you.'

The audience goggled. They looked more closely.

Then someone said, 'That's a boy.'

'He's got a costume on!' said someone else.

'He ain't a rat-monster at all!' came the voice of a third person, and with cries of disappointment and anger they called for their money back.

Mr Tapscrew, who was busy outside drumming up another crowd, came in hastily.

'Hush – yes – all right – understood – money back, certainly – just keep your voices down, ladies and gentlemen – here, Mrs Tapscrew'll give you the money out the back here – hush now . . .'

He ushered them grumbling and muttering, out of the booth, and then went back in to find Roger munching his rotten potato.

Mr Tapscrew bent down and hit him so hard the potato flew out of his hands, and he fell full length to the floor.

'What'd you do that for? Ain't you got no sense?

You keep your bloody trap shut, you little fool! How can a rat say "thank you"?'

Roger, his head ringing, didn't know what Mr Tapscrew meant about the trap. He had a vague idea that traps were bad for rats, but he couldn't make any sense of it. One thing he was sure about, though.

'I'm not a rat any more,' he said, struggling to sit up. 'I'm a boy now. Old Bob told me that good boys say thank you, so—'

'Damn your Bob, and damn your thank yous! You'll do as I tell you, you ungrateful skellum! After all I done for you – I pick you out the gutter – I give you a home and a useful occupation – you go and spoil it with your niminy-piminy "thank you"! You ain't supposed to *thank* 'em! You're supposed to snarl and snatch and threaten! You're supposed to be a Rat-Boy, not a choir boy!'

'Ah,' said Roger, his head beginning to hurt now, 'if I'd knowed that I'd've done it. When I got changed into a boy, that's when I found out about being good, so I was doing that. When I was a rat I never knew about being good. So now I got to be a good Rat-Boy, only that's hard.'

'Oh, shut up, you sanctimonious little mumper! Just remember – snarl and snatch and threaten. Else I'll pull your bloody nose off. Now the next lot of punters'll be in any minute, and I want 'em hor-rified and disgusted. See?'

He kicked Roger for good measure, and went out. Roger felt a choking sensation in his throat, almost like a hiccup, and it might have turned into a sob except that he thought Mr Tapscrew wouldn't approve. And he did want to be a good rat-boy, so he gathered up the biggest bit of the potato and crawled back into the sewer-pipe to wait for the next audience to come in.

All that day and all through the evening he snarled and snatched and threatened, and the people threw him bits of mouldy bread and chicken heads and scraps of rancid pork and banana skins and potato peelings and rotten fish, and exclaimed with revulsion when he ate them.

GOOSE WEATHER

After being St Matthew's, the fair moved on to a town fifty miles away to become the Goose Fair. At this time of year there were a lot of geese being fattened for Christmas, and autumn was getting on, so the evenings were longer and darker.

Mr Tapscrew was looking forward to good business, because people were more willing to come in out of the cold and look at an exhibition of curiosities than they were in the long summer evenings, when the rides and the merry-go-rounds did their best business. He paid for a new sign showing the Rat-Boy with an expression of savage malevolence, dripping green venom from hideous fangs. He even had special leaflets printed, and travelled ahead and distributed them in all the pubs.

As for Roger, he took to being a Rat-Boy quickly

enough, once he realized what he had to do; and he didn't mind what he ate, so the fish-heads and rotten carrots went down easily enough; but there wasn't any goodness in them, and presently he began to feel a little listless. He didn't enjoy swishing his tail any more, and the rat-suit was getting loose.

Mrs Tapscrew cursed, and took it in half an inch.

'He ain't eating his scraps,' she said to her husband, as they sat in their caravan. The lamplight was golden, the stove was warm, the kettle was singing. Outside, the rain was lashing at the windows, and the autumn wind was howling.

'Mmm,' said Mr Tapscrew, applying a match to his cigar and puffing luxuriously. 'Think we ought to feed him proper, then?' he said once it was nicely lit. 'Bit of soup of an evening?'

'Don't be daft. You know how the takings go up at feeding time. If he's full of soup and stuff, he won't be worth watching. No, I think you ought to hit him.'

'Well,' said Mr Tapscrew reluctantly, 'I could. The thing is,' he went on, examining the glowing tobacco, 'I don't think he's normal. I don't think he understands the meaning of things.'

'You're too soft,' she said, snapping off a thread between her teeth. 'You're getting attached to him. That's your problem. Like that blooming mermaid.

You were too interested in her by a long way—'

'All right, all right,' said Mr Tapscrew hastily. 'I'll do as you say, dear. I'm sure he'll settle down.'

Roger was trying to settle down at that very moment. He slept in his pit, curled up in the sewer pipe, and it was cold and draughty, and Mrs Tapscrew was sewing up his rat-suit, so he only had his tattered old page-boy uniform to keep out the cold. But he piled up some straw to keep out the worst of the wind, and nibbled a twig that someone had thrown in, and whispered the words he always whispered each night before he went to sleep: 'Bob and Joan – bread and milk – nightshirt – privy – patience.'

And soon afterwards he fell asleep.

But he hadn't been asleep for long when a knocking sound woke him up. It was coming from the wooden wall of the wagon, at the back of his sewer pipe. He turned round and pressed his ear to the wall, and there it was, knock-knock-knock – pause – knock-knock-knock.

And then there came a whisper through the cracks in the planks:

'Psst! Rat-Boy!'

Roger woke up properly.

'Yes?' he whispered back.

'Listen,' said the voice, 'I'm going to help you escape. In a minute I'm going to heave this plank out the way, and you can wriggle through.'

'Oh,' said Roger. 'Does Mr Tapscrew know?'

'No, and it's better if he doesn't,' said the voice. 'Keep it quiet now, Rat-Boy. Here goes.'

There was a crack and a splintering noise, and all of a sudden a cold wind blew in on Roger from a plank-wide gap in the wall. Amazed, he peered out and saw by the flickering light of a hurricane lantern a boy a little bigger than himself, with very pale hair that hung like a curtain over his forehead. Roger admired him enormously at once.

'Come on,' said the boy. 'Wriggle through. I bet you can.'

Roger was naturally a good wriggler, and his diet had left him so thin that he had no trouble at all in squirming through the gap. He fell on the muddy ground and got up at once.

'Come on,' said the boy. 'Let's run. We got to get away!'

'Yeah!' said Roger, joining in at once.

They ran along between the stalls, and then the other

boy turned and crouched in the shadows beside the ghost train, waiting to be sure the way was clear.

'Are you helping us all escape?' said Roger.

'Why, who else is there?' said the boy. 'I thought you was the only freak.'

'There's them,' said Roger, pointing up at the painted ghosts and skeletons of the ghost train. 'They're all locked in there like I was. We could let them out too.'

'You're a downy card, aintcher?' said the boy, looking both ways carefully. 'Right, come on!'

And he set off. Roger followed, looking back reluctantly at the still-imprisoned phantoms. Once they were safely in the darkness of the alleys under the castle, the boy stopped.

'Now,' he said. 'You call me Billy, understand?'

'Oh, yes, I understand,' said Roger. 'That's your name, Billy.'

'Yeah. Now I been watching you, Rat-Boy. I been in to look at your pit three times today, watching you wriggle. You probably didn't see me, but I was there. I'm on the lookout for a good wriggler, see, and I admired your style. I thought you wriggled like a champion. I got a job for you, Rat-Boy. So now you got to do as I tell you. Because I rescued you, and it's like you belong to me, you got to do everything I say.'

'Oh,' said Roger, nodding, 'I'll remember that.'

'Yes, you better. You're the lowest of the low, you are.'

'The lowest of the low,' said Roger proudly.

'That's right. Now listen, and I'll tell you something you never heard about. You listening?'

'Oh, yes,' said Roger, eager to learn.

'Look over there then,' said Billy, and pointed across the alley. Opposite them was a rusty iron gate with some broken spikes at the top, and through the gate the dismal gleam of a feeble gas lamp cast a glow over some weed-covered graves and broken tombstones.

'See that in there?' Billy whispered.

'Yeah. Looks nice. I bet there's—'

'Shut up. It don't look nice. It looks horrible. Scary, that's what it looks. That's where they bury all the dead people. Now real people, like me, we die natural. But rats, like you—'

'Ah,' said Roger, 'I ain't a rat any more. I'm a proper boy.'

'Once a rat, always a rat,' said Billy, and he said it with such simple certainty that it impressed itself on Roger profoundly. He struggled with it, but the words wouldn't go away. He said them to himself to make sure they were right, and Billy nodded.

'That's it,' he said. 'Now you interrupted me, and

I don't like that. Don't do it again. I was going to say that rats like you never die natural.'

'Don't we?'

'No. You got to be sterminated. If people think there's rats about, they send for the Sterminator. And if they even so much as suspect you're a rat underneath, watch out. The Sterminator'll be on his way.'

It sounded horrible. Roger gulped, and remembered the police sergeant: he had mentioned the Sterminator, too. He trembled and managed to say, 'What's it like?'

'It's not an it. It's a him. No-one's ever seen what he's like. He comes along with his apparatus and—'

The word 'apparatus' filled Roger with a deep and horrible dread. Terrifying pictures of a faceless man armed with some shadowy engine kept thrusting themselves into his mind, and he couldn't keep them out.

'No! Don't tell me!' he begged.

'Oh, I've got to, Roger,' Billy said gently. 'It wouldn't be right if I didn't tell you about the Sterminator. What he does with his apparatus—' Roger shivered and moaned – 'no-one knows, but when he's been sterminating, there ain't a single rat left to tell the tale. They find 'em with blood on their whiskers and their faces twisted with a nameless horror.'

'I ain't got whiskers,' said Roger, in faint hope.

'Wouldn't make no difference. The Sterminator, he can tell if someone's a rat underneath, even if they look like a boy in every particular.'

'Has there been other rats turned into boys, then?'

'Yeah. Doesn't happen often, but it has been known. The Sterminator's very hard on those cases. They're the ones he wants to sterminate most of all.'

'Like me,' whispered Roger, clutching himself with both arms.

'Just like you. It's a good thing you got me to look after you, innit? You do as I say and I'll keep the Sterminator off you. But you disobey me and I'll be so upset I'll forget. And the Sterminator'll have you while my back's turned, he's that quick.'

'Oh, no, don't forget,' Roger begged.

'Don't upset me, and I won't. Now you come along o' me and we'll find something good to eat. You hungry?'

Roger was now shaking so hard he felt his teeth chatter and his knees knock. He clenched his jaw and nodded, and gripped his knees to stop them, in case the sound attracted the Sterminator. There was a loose and swimmy sensation all around him.

'Follow me, then,' said Billy.

He led Roger down another alley, into a courtyard

lit only by the gleam on the wet cobbles, and lifted the lid of a coal chute. A faint glow came up, accompanied by the smell of frying.

'Down you go,' said Billy, shoving hard, and before he knew what was happening Roger had slid and tumbled on the dusty floor of a cellar, where a ring of glittering eyes surrounded him.

A hand reached out and snatched him off the floor a second before Billy tumbled down the chute behind him. Roger saw half a dozen boys, all bigger than he was, and all ragged and dirty. The glitter in their eyes came from an oil lamp and from the red-hot glow of a stove, on which one of the boys was frying chips.

'This is the Rat-Boy,' said Billy, dusting himself. 'You remember.'

'Oh yes,' said one boy, and, 'Aha,' said another, and, 'So this is him,' said a third.

Roger understood that the boys were glad to see him, and he did

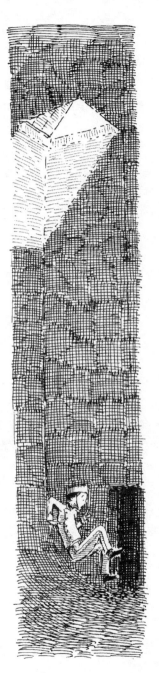

what he'd seen other people do, and held out his hand.

'How do you do,' he said to the first boy, and they all shook his hand one by one, laughing. They were so friendly altogether, squeezing his arms, pretending to look for his tail, fluffing up his hair, that he thought he'd never been happier; and then they gave him a hot chip and roared with laughter when he burned his mouth and dropped it on the floor, and he felt so grateful to them that his eyes filled with tears and he laughed even harder than they did.

WELL, WHERE'S HE GONE?

'Oh, the wickedness!' said Joan. 'We find him at last, and look at this!'

It was a cold grey morning. She held Bob's arm as they stood in the rainswept fairground, gazing up at the picture of the Rat-Boy and his venom-dripping fangs.

'Hold on,' said Bob, 'what's this?'

Joan peered closely at the notice pinned on the door of the wagon.

'*Due to unforeseen circumstances the world-famous Rat-Boy will not be appearing today. Exhibition closed until further notice. Open again SOON with even more amazing wonders. O. Tapscrew, Proprietor.*' Joan read it aloud. 'I hope Roger ain't fallen ill,' she said. 'Knock on the door and fetch this Tapscrew out, Bob.'

Bob knocked, and a minute later a harassed Mr Tapscrew opened it.

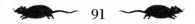

'Can't you read?' he said. 'The performance is cancelled.'

'Where is he?' said Bob.

'None of your business,' said Mr Tapscrew, and would have shut the door, except that Bob had his foot in it. 'Oy!' he went on. 'Go away!'

'You better listen to us,' said Bob, 'else we're going to the police.'

'Let 'em in,' said a voice from inside, a voice that sounded to Joan like lemon marmalade with too little sugar in it.

Mr Tapscrew opened the door, and Bob and Joan went in after him.

'Well?' he said.

'We want to know what you done with our Roger,' said Bob firmly.

'How d'you know he was yours?' said Mrs Tapscrew at once.

'We found a witness,' said Bob. 'We know you took him. You can't deny it. So where is he?'

'Wait a minute,' said Mrs Tapscrew. 'What's your interest in the Rat-Boy? You claiming to be his owners? You'd have to prove it.'

'Course we ain't his *owners*!' said Joan hotly. 'What d'you think he is, a slave, or a dog, or something?'

'Not his owners,' said Mrs Tapscrew. 'Then I

don't see what business it is of yours. Show them out, Oliver.'

'Oh no,' said Bob, and when he stood still, nothing on earth could budge him. 'You listen to me, and don't you talk till I've finished. That little boy come to us and we took him in. He didn't hardly know nothing, but he was a good little boy, and he tried hard to learn. But then he got lost, and that's the last we knew till we heard of you asking about Rat-Boys. He may be a Rat-Boy to you, and a handsome living, I don't doubt, but he don't belong here, he belongs in a home where he's going to be properly looked after. So where is he?'

'He's a freak,' said Mrs Tapscrew. 'Half rat, half human. He needs a profession. We was training him for a fine career. He could have been the best freak of all time. He could've been famous. He had the finest career in front of him that any freak's ever had. He could've—'

'What d'you mean, "freak"?' said Joan.

'What I say. He wasn't properly human. He couldn't have eaten all that filth otherwise. He was a—'

'Filth? What filth? What are you talking about?' said Joan.

Bob could feel her losing her temper, and he put his hand on her arm.

'Never mind the details,' he said. 'We want the main question, and the main question is, where is he?'

'He's gone,' said Mr Tapscrew.

'When?'

'Last night. He bust out of his wagon. Lovely warm wagon,' Mr Tapscrew said bitterly, 'with every sort of convenience, and he goes and smashes a plank out the side. That's going to cost me, that is. If you're responsible for him I shouldn't wonder if it ought to be you as pays for it.'

'You lock our little boy up and send us a bill when he escapes?' said Bob. 'Don't be daft. Let's go and look at this wagon.'

Joan was feeling strange. It was Bob saying 'our little boy'. He'd never said that before, and she'd never thought it, but now it was as if she was connected to Roger with the same sort of deep connection that joined her to Bob, and she felt herself saying it again in her head: our little boy.

Mr Tapscrew was reluctant to show them the wagon, because he had the idea that they wouldn't think it was quite as comfortable as he'd said, but he couldn't argue with Bob.

So grumpily he took his bunch of keys, and with Mrs Tapscrew coming as well to argue, they all trooped round to open the Rat-Boy's pit.

Joan waved her hand in front of her nose.

'You didn't keep him in here!' she cried.

'He wasn't very fastidious in his habits,' said Mrs Tapscrew.

'He didn't have anything to be fastidious in!' said Joan. 'And what's this? Is this what you gave him to eat?'

'No, no,' said Mr Tapscrew, shoving a piece of mouldy bread under a pile of straw with the side of his foot. 'We gave him lovely food – soup, stew – ever so nourishing. This was just professional food. A prop,' he added. 'That's what we call it. Props.'

'Slops, more like,' said Joan.

Bob was peering at the broken plank.

'He never done that,' he said to Mr Tapscrew. 'You're no workman, else you'd see in a moment. There's no leverage in here. Come outside.'

They went round the back, and Bob bent down and pointed to some marks on the next plank down.

'See that?' he said. 'That was a crowbar as done that. He never broke out. Someone broke in, and let him out.'

And he straightened up and faced Mr Tapscrew, and then suddenly prodded him in the chest with a forefinger that felt like a battering-ram. Mr Tapscrew staggered backwards.

'Oh – ah!—' he gasped. 'No need for assault—'

'You're responsible for this,' Bob said, and now his voice was like a battering-ram too, a very heavy one made of solid oak.

'No, not at all! Not a bit of it!' Mr Tapscrew blustered. 'We did everything we could to keep him safe and secure!'

'Well, *where's he gone?*'

THE SHARP ARTICLE

The boys in the cellar slept for most of the day, and so did Roger. When he woke up, he found Billy shaking him and holding some new clothes.

'Here,' said Billy, 'I got you some duds.'

'Did you just buy 'em?' said Roger, amazed at this generosity.

'You're a sharp article, and no mistake,' said Billy. 'I requisitioned 'em, that's what I did. Now slip them old togs off and put these on.'

When Roger proudly stood there in his new shirt and jacket he looked quite different from the tattered little page-boy he'd been. He looked like a sharp article, or a downy card.

'Now,' said Billy, 'you got to start earning a living. Me and my associates, we had a prime wriggler in the company, only he got too fat. And one day he set out a-wriggling and he got wedged. Course, there was nothing we could do. He was beyond our help. We had to leave him there.'

'Did the Sterminator get him?'

'I couldn't say. Maybe he didn't and maybe he did. But that wriggler weren't as good as you. You wouldn't get wedged.'

'No,' Roger agreed, shaking his head vigorously.

'Well, that's why you caught my eye in the fair. And when you wriggled out the wagon last night, that just made me even surer. You're a world-class wriggler, no doubt about it.'

Roger glowed.

'Am I going wriggling today?' he said.

'This evening,' said Billy. 'We're nocturnal. Like you, Rat-Boy. You're a nocturnal wriggler.'

'Yeah,' said Roger. 'That's what I am.'

The associates were just waking up. They all admired Roger's new duds, and soon there were eggs and slices of ham frying on the stove, and Roger was allowed a chunk of cheese as big as his two fists together, which kept him blissfully gnawing for a long time.

After they'd eaten, and when it was dark outside, Billy said, 'All right, lads. Line up.'

The associates stood in a row, and Billy

inspected them carefully. He checked their shoes (to make sure they didn't have metal bits on the heel that made a noise, or broken shoelaces that would trip them up), their clothes (to make sure they wore nothing light-coloured that would show up and give them away), and their sacks. Each boy carried a sack, and he had to hold it up and show Billy there was no hole in it.

'All present and correct,' Billy said. 'Good lads. Now we got a new wriggler, so we won't have the trouble we had last time. And as soon as we're done, straight back here by different routes. Just go through 'em, to show you remember. Dozzer first.'

A boy recited, 'Through the garden over the fence turn right along the canal over the bridge round the castle through the market and back home.'

'That's right,' said Billy, and each of the other boys recited his route, all different. Billy turned to Roger and said, 'That's the power of organization, see. As for you, you stick by me and you won't go wrong.'

Normally, he explained, they left the cellar by climbing a rope Billy had fixed by the coal chute, but he wanted to check Roger's wriggling one last time, so he pointed to a tiny window high up in a corner.

'See how long it takes you to get through that,' he

said. 'And mind, a good wriggler's got to be as quiet as a worm.'

'I can do that!' said Roger, and got through in less than half a minute, and waited excitedly for the others to climb the rope.

Presently all the boys were standing quietly in the alley. Billy patted each one on the back and sent them off at thirty-second intervals. It was so dark that even Roger's keen eyes couldn't see where they went.

REMOVALS

Half an hour later they were crouching in the bushes at the edge of a fine big garden looking up at the shuttered windows of a grand house.

'Now this is the problem, Roger,' Billy whispered. 'We got to get in, but there's only one way, and that's a loose airbrick over the scullery. But you could wriggle through there in a second, I bet.'

'Yeah, I bet too,' said Roger.

'Once you're inside,' Billy explained, 'you got to look around and find a key. Most folks are careless, and servants are specially careless. They don't like their masters and mistresses and they don't take trouble for 'em. So you look around, and ten to one you'll find a key on a hook somewhere, or a nail. Get that key and come and open the kitchen door.'

'I can do that!' said Roger. 'What are we going to do then? Are we going to live there?'

'No,' said Billy, 'the owners want us to do a removal job.'

Roger liked the sound of that, and said it to himself several times.

When everyone was ready, Billy said, 'Now, look closely at the wall just next to that little window and up a bit. There's a brick with holes in it there, what's called an airbrick. You take my crowbar – here it is – and get up on the window-sill, and jiggle it in beside the airbrick, and get it loose. When it comes out, you wriggle in and look for the key.'

Thrilled to be trusted with such complicated instructions, Roger took the crowbar from Billy. A few seconds later he was jiggling away at the crumbling mortar, and presently the airbrick did come loose. He passed it down to Billy, and then began to wriggle through.

It was a good thing he was a world-class wriggler, and probably a good thing too that he'd lost weight being the Rat-Boy, because several parts of him nearly got stuck. But even his widest bits were narrow, and what he remembered about being a rat helped too. It took him four whole minutes, but he got through in the end, to fall in a heap on the scullery floor, covered in dust and mortar.

'I done it!' he shouted. 'I got in!'

'Good boy,' said Billy outside, very quiet and calm.

The associates, hiding in the bushes, all heard Roger's shout, and their nerves were all twitching; but they felt a glow of admiration for the coolness of their leader as he just spoke softly and didn't move.

'Now you're in,' Billy was saying, 'you got to move around very quietly. That's the way we do removals. No noise. Now look for that key.'

A minute went by. Billy didn't move. Nor did the associates. Another minute went by. Then there was a little scrabbling noise at the back door, and Billy was there in a flash, turning the handle, and the door swung open.

The associates came tiptoeing over the flag-stones, making no more noise than a flock of shadows. Seconds after the door had begun to open, they were all in the big kitchen with the door shut again behind them.

'Well wriggled,' Billy said. 'Now, Roger, you stay here and keep watch. You know what to do, lads.'

The associates flitted away into the dark house. Roger stayed in the kitchen, wondering how to keep watch, but willing to do it, whatever it was.

Then, being Roger, he looked around for some-thing to eat.

Because the family who lived in the house had gone away, and taken their servants with them, there was no fresh food in the kitchen. But he found all kinds of dried food in jars and packets and boxes on the shelves. At first he thought he'd found some very long and very thin patience, but they tasted quite different from the wooden ones and snapped more easily, sending bits of themselves flying all over the kitchen. If he could have read the packet, it would have told him he was eating spaghetti.

When he'd had enough of that, he found some dried figs at the back of a shelf. Then he ate his way through a packet of cream crackers, one old and flexible carrot, half a pound of rice, and some very tasty dried beans.

Then he made a big mistake.

There was a paper bag twisted up in a corner, with some light rattling things in it, and Roger automatically thrust them all into his mouth and chewed and swallowed. Of course, he'd never heard of chillies, and never suspected what these were. They took a moment to hit.

Then he gasped and goggled and began to run around in circles, flapping at his mouth in the hope of cooling it down. He couldn't imagine what it was he'd eaten. His lips and his tongue and his throat and his stomach were all ablaze. Parts of his insides he'd never known about were sizzling. He yelped – he jumped – he squeaked – he gargled – he hooted – and suddenly the thought came to him: Water! Water! Water!

He ran to the tap, but the water was cut off at the mains, and only a hollow rattle filled his scorching mouth. He was making all kinds of noises now – mewlings and whinnyings and yippings and hoick-ings and gurkings – and then he remembered the big barrel that stood just outside the kitchen door. He'd seen it on the way in.

He tore outside and scrambled up between the barrel and the wall, only to find a big wooden lid at the top. He hauled it off in desperation, dropping it to the cobbles with a crash, and plunged his whole head into the cold wet delicious moon-reflecting depths.

Gripping the barrel with both hands, feet pressed hard to the slippery sides, Roger swallowed and guzzled and swallowed and gulped. Oh, the relief! The marvellous coolness! The sweet wetness of his mouth! He swallowed till he was just about waterlogged.

As full as he could be, he loosened his grip and slid down the side of the water-butt. And he forgot all about his burning mouth and turned his attention downwards, for something strange was happening inside him. He staggered slightly on the ground and listened to his stomach. All kinds of burblings and gurglings and swooshings and bubblings were taking place, as the cascade of water met the dried beans and the rice and sloshed about among the bits of spaghetti. Roger felt his turbulent belly with apprehensive hands. As the grains of rice began to swell, and the dried beans began to soak up the water and double in size, as the bits of pasta grew plump and fat, Roger's stomach began to strain at the buttons of his new shirt, creaking and rumbling.

'Oh,' he said, staggering a bit, 'ah. Ooh.' Then he said, 'Hic!'

He'd never had hiccups before. He thought he was exploding. He clenched his teeth together to stop it, but the next *hic* simply came out through his nose instead. And all the time his stomach was getting fuller and fuller and fatter and fatter.

He staggered this way and that, gulping, hicking, gasping, snorting, feeling very sorry for himself indeed.

And suddenly a light shone into his eyes, and a hand closed over his shoulder, and a deep voice said, 'What's going on here?'

WHO'S THAT?

Above them, in a window overlooking the scullery yard, several pairs of eyes glittered silently and then withdrew.

Roger, dazed and bloated, could hardly think. But when he looked up and saw the policeman looming against the sky, he knew there was only one person it could be.

'Billy! Help!' he yelled. 'It's the Sterminator! Come and help me!'

And he sank his teeth into the policeman's hand.

The man gasped and let him go, to seize the truncheon at his waist, but Roger was out of reach already and running about in fear, looking up at the house and calling, 'Billy! Billy! Come and fight him!'

'More of you, are there?' said the policeman. 'Like rats in a trap.'

And he blew his whistle. That was enough for Roger. If the man spoke of rats, he must be the Sterminator, and the whistle must be his horrifying apparatus starting up. For all his loyalty to Billy, and despite his waterlogged stomach, the little boy turned and fled into the dark.

He didn't know where he was going. He couldn't remember the way back to the cellar, and even if he could, he didn't dare go there. In fact, everything in his world was soaked in guilt and misery. He had wanted to be a good boy, but it seemed that whatever he did, he was a bad one. He didn't deserve a nice dry place to curl up and sleep; he didn't even deserve to whisper *Bob and Joan – bread and milk – nightshirt – privy – patience* as he used to do.

Somehow the words didn't want to come to his mouth. He just moved his lips and tried to hear the little puffs and clicks and hisses they made and pretended he could make out the words.

So he crept through the dark streets until he came to a grating in the gutter, like a proper rat-hole, only human-sized. If he went down there he wouldn't have to bother anyone and he wouldn't do anything wrong. He could stop trying to be a boy and go back to being a rat. 'Once a rat, always a rat,' Billy had told him, and it must be true, because he certainly wasn't any good at being a boy.

So he lifted the grating and slipped down into the dark.

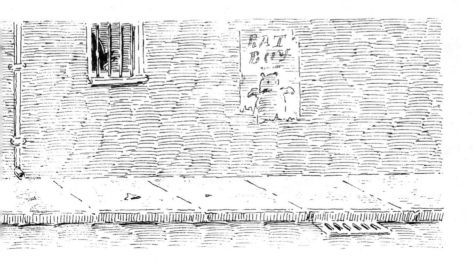

The Daily Scourge

CRIME UP AGAIN

This is becoming a crime-ridden country – and it's official.

Crime figures have risen for the fifth year in succession.

Typical of the sort of lawlessness all too common today is the break-in at the home of the Earl and Countess of Ditchwater by a gang of young boys, all of whom were luckily caught red-handed.

'I blame the teachers,' said the Home Secretary.

'Ere, 'ere!

Rotten to the core

ANARCHY IN THE CLASSROOMS

But teachers are finding it harder and harder to maintain order and discipline over the bullies and thugs in the classroom.

'There is no respect for learning any more,' said a teachers' leader. 'I blame the parents.'

FAMILY BREAK-UPS

The traditional family is under threat. Family values have crumbled away. Changing working patterns, taxation, and violent entertainment are playing havoc with all the old certainties.

'There's no-one to give a moral lead any more,' said a parent. 'I blame the church.'

A MORAL VACUUM

But the church itself speaks with an uncertain voice.

'How can anyone be moral in a world of poverty under the constant threat of war and environmental devastation?' said the Archbishop. 'I blame the government.'

THE SCOURGE SAYS:

RUBBISH!

All our so-called experts are wrong, as usual.

Dripping and moaning about the state of the world and blaming everyone else – is it any wonder that our country is in a mess, with people like that in charge of it?

As for the rise in juvenile crime, it's easy.

The kids are doing it, aren't they?

Then there's no need to look any further.

BLAME THE KIDS!!!

The Daily Scourge READERS OFFER!

MECHANICAL GUARD DOG

ONLY £499·99!

ELECTRIC FENCE ONLY £2,799!

HEAVILY ARMED GARDEN GNOME ONLY £299·99!

PATIO TRAP DOOR ONLY £1,599·99!

A PAIR OF OLD TRAMS

The fair had moved on. Mr Tapscrew had dismantled the Rat-Boy's Pit of Horror, and Mrs Tapscrew, with the aid of some horsehair and glue, had become a Bearded Woman to keep up the cash flow. She'd do it for a week and that was it, she said, it was too itchy for any more than that; so Mr Tapscrew was trying to persuade the Dodgems' sulky daughter to become Serpentina, the Snake-Girl. The Rat-Boy was over and done with.

Meanwhile, Bob and Joan had had to go back home, because there was work to be done, and they'd run out of money. They had to spend a few days earning some more, and then they went back to the town where the fair had been, and looked around.

They spent all day at it. They asked in every

shop, they looked in every alley, they even did what they'd been uneasy about before and went to the police.

But the police were no help. The sergeant on duty took down the details and promised to have a poster made up, but without a picture, he pointed out, they couldn't expect much.

Bob and Joan went to sit in the Memorial Gardens to have their sandwiches.

'I feel as if we'll never find the poor little scrap,' she said.

'No,' said Bob, 'we'll find him. Don't fret, old girl. You know what?'

'What?'

'I reckon we got a purpose in our lives now, that's what. We been just trundling along all these years like a pair of old trams. I didn't think about nothing except soles and heels and the price of leather. But when that little boy come and knocked on our door, I got a jolt, I did. And now he's vanished I don't want to go trundling on in a straight line all the way to me grave. I got something better to do. Are you with me, old girl?'

'You're a silly old man,' she said. 'You and your trams. Who are you calling a tram? How long have we been married now? I bet you can't remember.'

'Thirty-two years,' he said.

'Well all right, you can remember. And you have the nerve to ask if I'm with you. If I wasn't with you all the way to the depot, Bob Jones, I'd have gone off a long time ago. When you were talking to that Tapscrew, and you said – it was when you said – oh dear—'

She cried a bit then, and Bob just held her hand and let her dab her eyes.

'It was when you said "our little boy",' she went on after a bit, 'that's what done it. I'd go anywhere now and do anything to fetch him home, I really would. But oh, Bob . . . Do you really think he was a rat? That ain't possible, is it, for a rat to become a real boy?'

'No,' he said. 'Least, I never heard of it, or read it in the paper.'

'You and your blooming paper. Then what do you think *is* the truth about it? He wasn't lying, was he?'

'No. He's a truthful little soul. I don't think he could ever tell a lie. Even when he done bad things he owned up straight away. And they weren't really bad things anyway, only the kind of things a poor innocent beast would do . . .'

'Like a rat,' she said.

'That's right. I don't like rats any more than the next bloke, but they ain't wicked and cruel like people can be. They're just ratty in their habits.'

'That's Roger, too. Just a bit ratty in his habits,' she repeated, and dabbed her nose. 'There, I'm a bit better now. Oh, it is a worry . . .'

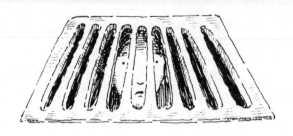

HUNCHED AND MALEVOLENT, RADIATING PURE EVIL

The paper Bob read was good for sport, Bob said, but he usually read the stories about lottery winners and scandals and murders as well, and so did hundreds of thousands of other people.

The editor of the *Daily Scourge* encouraged his reporters to listen out for every kind of weird, or sentimental, or horrible, or sensational story they could find, and then he printed them, whether or not they were true. The best kind of story was one that went on and on, with a new twist every day, and could be easily understood even by numskulls in a hurry.

The *Daily Scourge* hadn't found much in the way of that kind of story recently. They had tried to whip up some interest in the royal wedding, but as soon as that was over people stopped buying so many papers. The editor was getting impatient.

So when an ambitious young *Daily Scourge* reporter began to hear a strange kind of rumour, he pricked up his ears and started asking questions. Pretty soon, more rumours began to circulate. There were said to be ghosts in the drains: people had heard them whispering. Someone had seen a creepy face looking up at her from a rainwater grating. And the men who cleaned the sewers swore they'd seen something down there in the dark.

The reporter arranged to meet three of the sewage workers in a pub, and bought them lots of drinks.

'So what is all this then?' he said. 'You saw something in the sewers? What sort of thing?'

'Something uncanny,' said one. 'A ghost, I reckon.'

'Or an evil spirit,' suggested another.

'A hobgoblin, even,' said the third man.

'What's it look like?'

'Ooh, evil,' said the first man. 'I couldn't describe it. I been working down the sewers all me life, and I never been frightened till now.'

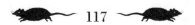

'I tell you,' said the second man, 'it's not a fit sight for human eyes, what we saw down there.'

'A little figure,' said the third man, 'sort of like a horrible little man, scampering, running, kind of thing. Not like a proper human being. Kind of hunched and malevolent.'

Hunched and malevolent, the reporter wrote in his notebook. 'Good,' he said. 'What else?'

'You know where I seen something like that before?' said the second man. 'In the carving on the cathedral doorway showing the sinners being hauled off down the pit. There's a devil there with just the exact same expression. Gives you the shivers. Just radiating pure evil.'

Pure evil, wrote the reporter. 'Brilliant,' he said.

'And I tell you something else,' said the first man. 'The rats is back.'

'Rats?'

'Thousands and thousands of 'em. They cleared 'em out not so long ago, but they come back with a vengeance. You can hear 'em twittering in the dark. They're follering this ghost about.'

'Fantastic!' said the reporter. 'Look, lads, I don't suppose I could get down there and have a look around?'

They looked doubtful. He took out his wallet. They nodded.

The Daily Scourge

MONSTER FOUND IN SEWERS

by our Star Reporter, Kelvin Bilge

A monster, semi-human in shape, has been found living in the city's sewers.

It was captured yesterday after a desperate struggle in which three sewage workers were badly wounded.

HUNDREDS MORE

Experts believe that the monster is the first of a new breed.

'There could be hundreds more breeding down below us,' said a scientist. 'The only solution is to destroy them before they get too strong for us.'

EXTERMINATION

The monster is being kept in the custody of the quarantine department so that scientists can examine it before it is

Manhole where daring **Scourge** *reporter, Kevin Bilge, entered sewers to confront monster*

exterminated.

The Mayor and City Council were urged last night to waste no more time.

OUTRAGE AT MERCY PLEA

There was outrage when some politicians urged caution.

'We should not rush to judgement,' said an Opposition spokesman. 'The Monster is a victim too.'

THE FREEDOM OF THE PRESS

All over the country, people read the *Daily Scourge* and shuddered.

In fact there was such a stir about the Monster of the Sewers that other stories vanished altogether. No-one was interested in the Chancellor's income-tax proposals, or in the Prince's return from his honeymoon with his new Princess, or even in the sports results: everyone wanted to hear about the Monster.

The *Daily Scourge* printed a special weekend supplement, and sold an extra two hundred and fifty thousand copies as a result.

Special Supplement

THE MONSTER OF THE SEWERS

Scientists are baffled by this creature. Is it the relic of a lost tribe of subhuman creatures?

Is it a visitor from another world?

Or is it a hideous mutation caused by environmental pollution?

What is certain is that nothing like it has ever been discovered before.

Its evil and bloodthirsty past can only be guessed at.

We must be thankful that the vigilance of the *DAILY SCOURGE* has revealed this horrible threat to the public.

Artist's impression of the evil monster in his lair in the sewers.

YOUR VOTE

Fill in this coupon and send it to us:

Should this evil monster be destroyed?

YES

NO

DON'T BE DECEIVED

At the quarantine department, the Government Chief Scientist looked in at the creature through the bars of the cage. It sat in a heap of straw, looking back at him with an expression which, of course, he couldn't understand.

'Certainly anthropoid,' he said, and his assistant made a note. 'I've heard talk of some connection with rats, but there's nothing rodent in its physiology, to my mind.'

'It's done a fair bit of gnawing,' said his assistant.

'So do chimpanzees. Twigs and things. This is a form of ape, no doubt about it.'

'But what was it doing in the sewers?'

'That's what we shall have to find out.'

The Chief Scientist was there because the Prime Minister had sent him to investigate. The Prime

Minister was taking a close interest in the Monster case, because he wasn't very popular just then, and nor were any of the ministers in the government. It was a great help to have something else on the front pages of the papers, and even better to have something new for the public to hate. So the Chief Scientist was under instructions to find the Monster as loathsome as possible, and to spin out the examination for as long as he could.

With two experienced zookeepers at hand, armed with nets and prods in case the Monster became dangerous, the Chief Scientist opened the cage and went inside. His assistant stayed close at hand to make notes.

The Monster didn't look very monstrous, but the Chief Scientist didn't go by surface appearances. It was what lay underneath that mattered. This little shivering naked thing might have had the form of an ape, or even (to be more accurate) a human boy, but that only made it more horrible and unnatural. The Chief Scientist wrinkled his nose and prodded the creature with a pencil.

At once the Monster made a semi-human noise

and seized the pencil in its filthy paw. The Chief Scientist let go, alarmed, and the Monster began to nibble the pencil with every appearance of pleasure.

'Remarkable,' said the Chief Scientist. 'Certainly an anthropoid manner of gnawing. Must be conditioned. Couldn't be inborn. Teeth the wrong shape altogether.'

'Excuse me, sir,' said one of the zookeepers uncertainly. 'Did I get it wrong, or did he say *Thank you?*'

The Chief Scientist laughed indulgently.

'No, no,' he said, 'the sound you heard was purely a reflex vocalization. It was your mind that put any meaning into it. I want you to hold the creature still so I can take a sample of its blood.'

'We better use the net, sir,' said the zookeeper.

'Go on then. I shall need a fore-limb so I can find a vein.'

The zookeepers threw their net over the Monster, which struggled violently, uttering lots of reflex vocalizations. But everyone disregarded them now, knowing that they didn't mean anything, and presently the creature was trussed and pinioned on the straw, with its forelimb outstretched.

'Hold it tight,' said the Chief Scientist, and stuck a needle into the skinny little arm and drew off some blood.

The creature howled and kicked and cried, but they found it was easier if they took no notice. The Chief Scientist corked the little bottle.

'That'll do for today,' he said. 'Now as for food: I've drawn up a list here, and I want it fed twice a day according to the plan. Then we'll try different kinds of stimulus to see what it responds to. Firstly we'll try noise. Then we'll lower the temperature . . .'

His assistant wrote all the plans down dutifully.

'He does seem . . . I don't know . . . very human,' she said tentatively when he'd finished.

'Appearances are only superficial. I expect to find the creature quite different, underneath, from what it seems on the surface.'

'Yes,' she said.

Our Children Are In Danger

The results of the *Daily Scourge*'s Readers' Poll came in: 96% said the Monster should be destroyed, 2% said it shouldn't, and 2% didn't know, which was clever of them, because there wasn't a box to tick for *don't know*. The publicity campaign was building up. Other papers joined in.

Every minute this vile and savage monster remains alive, said one paper, *our children are in danger*.

When is the government going to act? said another.

Make the streets safe for our children! said a third.

Before long, the Monster was the main topic of conversation and guesswork. Everyone had an opinion, and the less they knew, the more strongly they expressed themselves. Soon politicians began

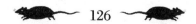

to speak up as well. An MP said in Parliament, 'It is time to do away with old-fashioned scruples! There are choices that are hard, options that are painful, courses of action that require resolution and courage, but we must not shrink from the task, we must not falter, we must be bold and determined! I say to you, we must carry out this duty, and do so with a firm and fearless hand!'

What that meant was: we must do exactly what the *Daily Scourge* tells us to do, and hope it'll be nice to us. And what *that* meant was: we must get someone to kill the Monster. But of course he wouldn't have said it openly, because it sounded rather brutal, put like that.

Even the Government spent most of their cabinet meetings talking about the Monster.

'The public is alarmed!' said the Home Secretary. 'We must do something to calm their fears!'

'Stuff and nonsense,' said the Chancellor of the Exchequer. 'I don't believe this Monster even exists.'

'Well, it does, and I've seen it,' said the Minister for Agriculture.

They were amazed. 'How did you manage that?' said the Foreign Secretary, enviously.

'The quarantine department is my responsibility. And I have to tell you that when you see the Monster in the flesh, it looks uncannily like a small boy.'

'Appearances are deceptive!' said the Minister for Education.

'You can't judge by appearances!' said the Lord Chancellor.

'It's what's underneath that matters, not what it looks like on the surface!' said the Home Secretary. 'And I say the public demand a firm hand! This thing should be exterminated!'

'Well, normally, one would agree,' said the Minister of Agriculture. 'But consider the problem from the point of view of presentation. What would it look like to take what appears to be a small child and, as you say, exterminate him?'

There was a silence at that. They all saw the problem.

'Perhaps we could dress him up to look more like a monster,' suggested the Minister of Education. 'It wouldn't look so bad then.'

They talked for hours. It was clear that they had to do something, or the newspapers would turn all their fury against them. But whatever they did mustn't seem unjust, because you could never tell what the voters would put up with, and there was an election coming up in a year or so.

Only the Prime Minister kept quiet. And when they asked him what he thought, he had an answer ready.

'I think we ought to set up a tribunal under a High Court judge, and call expert witnesses and so on, and let that decide,' he said firmly.

'Excellent idea!'

'A brilliant solution!'

'Magnificent stroke of imagination!'

They all agreed. So they appointed a judge, and set a date, and announced that the fate of the Monster was going to be decided by law.

TRIPE

On the day before the tribunal was going to begin, Bob and Joan were sitting at home, exhausted. They'd just come back from hours and hours of knocking on doors at the other end of town, just asking if anyone had seen Roger, because they couldn't think what else to do; and when they got back there was a load of washing to do and seven pairs of shoes to be re-soled and heeled; and now it was nearly midnight and they were drinking a cup of cocoa before going to bed.

Bob listlessly picked up the paper. He hadn't read it for days, and although he'd seen the headlines about monsters, he couldn't be bothered to read them: all he was interested in was Roger. But in order to take his mind off their trouble, he'd bought a copy on the way home, and he began to

read the main story wearily. Then he sat up.
    'Here,' he said, 'listen to this.'
    He rustled the paper and began to read.

The Daily Scourge

FURY OVER MONSTER 'EXPERTS'

There was widespread fury today at reports that some so-called scientists will testify on behalf of the Rat-Monster at the Tribunal tomorrow.

The 'defence' intends to make the absurd claim that the subhuman creature from the darkness is actually a human being and should be spared extermination.

HELPLESS VICTIMS

Members of the public were quick to condemn this move.

'How can we sleep safely when this hideous evil beast is still alive?' said Mrs Kitty Nettles, 38.

Mrs Nettles is a mother of six.

Six adorable, helpless children. Children who might be victims of the ravening fiend.

Mrs Kitty Nettles, 27, and her family sheltering in an emergency refuge from gigantic, marauding, evil hell-monster

EVIL BEYOND BELIEF

Parents' groups were forming protest committees last night.

'This monster is evil beyond belief,' said Mr Derek Pratt, 46. 'Something must be done to protect our kiddies from the monster demon from hell. The government are keeping him safe on purpose. It is a conspiracy to protect the criminal elements and put ordinary innocent people into danger. If the government does not act to destroy this foul beast then we shall keep our children home from school indefinitely.'

RIOT OVER HUNCHED FIGURE

A 500-strong crowd attacked a police station with bricks and stones after rumours spread that the Monster was inside.

'I saw this horrible hunched figure being taken in the back,' said Mrs Glenda Brain, 57. 'It was entirely covered in a blanket but I knew it was the Monster. I just had a feeling.'

THE SCOURGE SAYS:

If the government does not act soon there will be bloodshed and it will be their fault.

KILL THE MONSTER NOW.
BEFORE IT'S TOO LATE!

'What you reading that tripe for?' said Joan. 'That ain't worth using to wipe your feet on, that rubbish.'

'No, listen,' said Bob. 'We been so busy we missed all this. It seems they found this rat-creature in the sewers, and they're going to put it on trial and decide whether or not to kill it.'

Joan realized what he meant.

'You don't think—' she began.

'No, it couldn't be,' he said reluctantly. 'But just suppose—'

'What's it look like?'

'Let's see,' said Bob, turning the page. 'Evil –

hideous – dangerous – vile – bloodthirsty – they don't say what it looks like . . .'

'He couldn't *change*, could he? The little one? He couldn't go back to being a proper rat?'

Bob was silent. 'We don't know as he ever was,' he said finally. 'He might have only thought it.'

'Bob, suppose it *is* Roger?' she said. 'And they're going to kill him!'

'Well, we'll have to go and stop 'em,' he said.

No Room

The court building was crowded, and Bob and Joan had to struggle through packed corridors before they found the courtroom; and then they couldn't get in.

'Quite impossible,' said the usher outside the door. 'We been full up since seven o'clock this morning.'

'Please!' said Joan. 'We *got* to find out what this monster is!'

'So's ten thousand other people. Why should I let you in?'

'All right,' said Bob, 'here, take this. Here's a pound for you.'

'Get away!' the usher laughed. 'A *pound*? You're joking! *Fifty* pounds, and I might look the other way while you slip in at the back. There's some as gave me a hundred for a seat near the front. A *pound*? I'm insulted. Clear off.'

Bob would have had to go home on foot if the usher had taken the bribe, because it was all he had for the bus fare. Now he felt humiliated.

Joan said, 'There's no need to be rude, young man. What are all these people doing here if *they* can't get in?'

'Witnesses,' said the usher, and turned away to keep someone else out.

Joan tugged at Bob's arm and whispered, 'Those scientists must be here then – from the paper – the ones who are going to defend him . . .'

Bob unfolded the page he'd torn from the paper.

'Doesn't say their names, though,' he said.

'Perhaps we could find them,' she said hopefully.

The people in the corridor were arguing loudly and showing one another papers and diagrams and models of bones and skulls.

The door opened, and the usher called loudly:

'Mr Kelvin Bilge! Calling Mr Kelvin Bilge!'

One of the witnesses got up and followed him out.

'They must have started the trial,' said Bob.

He and Joan sat down unobtrusively near one of the loudest-arguing groups, and listened to what they were saying.

'—and it was surrounded by rats! Thousands of them!'

'—carry plague—'

'—assistant swore she'd heard it say *thank you*! I ask you!'

Bob and Joan looked at each other.

'—reflex vocalizations—'

'—studies on the vocal tract of parrots—'

'—particular fondness for pencils—'

Bob and Joan held each other's hand tightly.

'—of course the outcome's all arranged already, they're going to put it down—'

'*Daily Scourge*—'

'—I understand it sleeps curled up very small—'

Bob couldn't sit still. Joan got up with him and they walked to the end of the corridor and back, unable to speak.

Then the door opened. The usher looked out and called 'Mr Gordon Harkness! Calling Mr Gordon Harkness to the witness stand!'

No-one responded.

'Mr Gordon Harkness, please!'

Suddenly an idea came to Bob. He squeezed Joan's hand.

'Oh, sorry,' he called out. 'Mr Harkness, yes, that's me!'

'What are you *doing*?' Joan whispered.

'It's the only way to get in!' he whispered back.

'This way, please,' said the usher.

Bob tugged at Joan's reluctant hand. She was sure he'd be arrested for impersonation, and then they'd be in even more trouble, but he was just as solid and fearless as he ever was, and he said to the usher. 'This is my wife, Mrs Harkness. She's a witness too. I can't give me testimony without her. She's got to come in with me.'

'She's not on my list,' said the usher.

'That's because she weren't available. She was away seeing her niece. But she is now, so she ought to be with me.'

'Oh, very well. I don't suppose it matters.'

And the usher showed them into the courtroom.

THE TRIBUNAL

There was a rustle of surprise all round the crowded court as Bob and Joan walked up to the witness stand together. Joan looked around nervously: there was a judge with a wig and a red gown, and rows of lawyers with wigs and black gowns, and what looked like hundreds of people crammed onto benches and standing at the back. To keep herself from trembling, Joan tried to count the seated ones and multiply by a hundred, and the standing ones and multiply by fifty, and add them together, to see how much money the usher had made.

As soon as Bob and Joan were on the stand, a lawyer stood up clutching his lapels and said, 'You are Mr Gordon Harkness, Lecturer in Comparative Anatomy?'

'No, I ain't,' said Bob. 'I'm Bob Jones, cobbler. And this is my wife Joan, washerwoman.'

'Then what are you doing here?'

'I had to pretend,' Bob went on, 'because you wouldn't have let us in otherwise. We got information about this so-called Monster that you ought to hear.'

The crowd was buzzing with excitement and curiosity. Lawyers passed notes to one another, the reporters scribbled busily, and all the spectators were talking and pointing and standing up to look.

'Silence!' said the Judge. 'I will have order in this court room. If we don't have silence, I shall clear the court.'

Everybody suddenly stopped talking.

'Now, Mr Jones,' said the judge, 'if that is your name, you had better explain yourself. This is a serious matter.'

'All right, your lordship,' said Bob. 'You see, we

reckon that this Monster ain't a monster at all. It's a little boy called Roger. And all you need to do is just fetch him here and let everyone look at him, and if it is him, then we'll take him home and that'll be an end of it.'

'Is this Roger a relation of yours?' said the Judge. 'A child or a grandchild?'

'Well, no.'

'Then what is your connection with him?'

'He just knocked on the door one night and we took him in,' Bob explained.

'Did you try to find out where he came from?'

'Yes.'

'Well, what did he tell you?'

'He said he'd been a rat,' said Bob unhappily.

The Judge glared at him.

'He did, Your Honour,' said Joan.

He glared at her too. Some of the people began to

whisper, and some began to laugh. The judge banged his gavel for silence.

'And what did you do with this child?' he asked.

'We took him to the police, to the hospital, to the City Hall, and none of 'em wanted him. We sent him to school and all they did was thrash him. Then a gentleman called the Philosopher Royal called and took him away for some tests, and he frightened the boy and he ran away. Since then we been looking all over for him.

'And every time we nearly found him, something happened and he ran off somewhere else. He's a friendly little feller but he's very easy to mislead. And when we heard of this Monster nonsense we thought we should come along, in case they exterminated him by mistake.'

'I see,' said the Judge. 'Is the Philosopher Royal due to attend as a witness?'

'Tomorrow, my lord,' said the Clerk of the Court.

'Send for him now,' said the Judge. 'Mr and Mrs Jones, you did a wrong thing in deceiving the court. Nevertheless, I accept that you acted for what you thought were good reasons, and I direct that you shall be found room to sit and listen to the rest of the tribunal. But whether you are called again to the witness stand depends on my judgement.'

'Thank you, my lord,' said Bob.

The usher led them to a bench at the front and made everyone else squeeze up, which led to a lot of grumbling.

By this time the real Mr Harkness had arrived, and he was brought in next. He had examined the Monster, he claimed, and discovered all kinds of ways in which it was non-human. He showed the court diagrams and charts and mathematical tables, and proved by the use of chemical analysis and statistical spectroscopy that the Monster was an unknown and dangerous life-form.

Bob began to fidget. Joan nudged him to keep still.

The next witness was someone surprising: none other than Mr Tapscrew. Bob sat up and clenched his fists.

'You are the proprietor of a fairground exhibition?' said the lawyer.

'I am, sir, and proud to be so,' said Mr Tapscrew.

'Please tell the court of your involvement with the Monster.'

'I have had long experience with the freak trade, my lord. I have exhibited numerous natural wonders, from the famous Sumatran mermaid to the Boneless Wonder of Mexico.

'Now I don't need to explain to you sophisticated ladies and gentlemen that much of the business of a fairground exhibition is in the nature of light-hearted make-believe. My mermaid, for instance – well, whether there's mermaids in the sea I couldn't say, but this one was a girl called Nancy Swillers, and her tail was run up out of satin and sequins by my good lady wife. Mind you, we did good business with her; the patrons got their money's worth, Nancy got a wage, everyone was satisfied.

'But I'm always on the lookout for new and unusual exhibits to set before the public, my lord. And when I heard of a new kind of a monster, half child, half rat, I set out to find it. And—'

'One moment, Mr Tapscrew,' said the judge. 'Where did you hear of this phenomenon?'

'In the saloon bar of a pub called the Black Horse, if I remember right,' said Mr Tapscrew. 'I was passing the time of day, and someone happened to mention that he'd heard tell of a creature very like a child, only different, really a rat, in fact, being looked after or concealed by some neighbours of his. And this creature would gnaw its way through anything – it was wild, it was dangerous, it was probably carrying all kinds of diseases – he wasn't happy about living next to it.'

'Charlie,' muttered Bob.

'Sssh!' said Joan.

'Well, following on from this,' Mr Tapscrew went on, 'I made enquiries and began to investigate, and being a determined and experienced investigator, I soon found the creature in question.'

'Did you take it back to its carers? These neighbours you mentioned?' asked the lawyer.

'No. The fact was, I didn't know this man's name, the chap in the pub, and I forgot where he'd told me he lived. So—'

'I thought you said you were an experienced investigator,' said the Judge.

'You're quite right, my lord,' said Mr Tapscrew cheerfully, not a bit put out. 'So I did. But it was very late at night when I found it, and the rat-creature itself seemed to form an attachment to me. Anyway, he wouldn't leave me, and I took him home out of pure charity and my good lady wife gave him a meal and as we watched him eat, the idea came to me of exhibiting him as an educational display.

'So we went to great expense to fit out a wagon full of all the most comfortable surroundings, and made sure he had the most varied food, and opened it up to the serious-minded and discerning public.

'And I have to say, my lord—' here Mr Tapscrew took out an enormous handkerchief and blew his nose vigorously, '—I have to say we became quite attached to the creature, very fond indeed. It would curl up at our feet of an evening and take food from our hands, and we even taught it a few words.'

He dabbed his eyes, 'But nature will out, my lord,' he said sadly. 'You can take the beast into your home, but you can't make him human. One day the creature treacherously gnawed through the side of his wagon and escaped, and we haven't seen him from that day to this.'

Bob could hardly contain himself. Every muscle in his body was twitching to get up and punch Mr Tapscrew on his lying nose, but he knew that if he did that he'd be thrown out, and Joan was squeezing his hand so tight her nails were digging into his palm.

'From your first-hand observations of the creature,' the lawyer was saying, 'did you draw any conclusions as to its nature?'

'Yes,' said Mr Tapscrew. 'For all his mimicking, he wasn't human. There was a definite scaliness about him. He was covered in scabs and pustules. I dread to think of the health risks, but my dedication to science is so great that I didn't worry about it. And his gnawing: that was the give-away. Just exactly like a giant rat. That and the pustules.'

'And from your experience, Mr Tapscrew, would you say that a creature of this sort could be successfully tamed?'

'No, sir, it could not. As a young one, what you might call a cub or a puppy kind of thing, it might display signs of human-style behaviour and even affection. But let 'em grow up and feel their strength, and soon they start growing wild. They want to dominate, you see, they won't be tamed. They ain't like your dogs, or your cats, what are proper domesticated pets. This is a wild and ferocious creature. Just let it get big enough and nothing'll stop it from tearing your throat out and chewing it up before your very eyes. With relish,' he added with relish.

'And you have no idea what happened to the Monster after it escaped?'

'None, your worship.'

'What are you exhibiting at the moment, Mr Tapscrew?'

'A very fine and unusual display, if I may say so, your lordship. Serpentina the Snake Girl. Half snake, half human, this lithe and sinister creature displays her uncanny—'

'Is she genuine? Or is she like your mermaid?'

'Aha, you're no fool, I can see that. No,' said Mr Tapscrew jovially, 'she's a bit of light-hearted amusement. Half price today, ladies and gentlemen! Half-price admission to the Snake Girl during the trial—'

'Thank you, Mr Tapscrew. You may stand down.'

As Mr Tapscrew left the witness stand, he handed out leaflets to the nearest people, until he saw Bob and Joan glaring at him. Then he looked the other way, and hurried out.

The usher was handing the Judge a note. The Judge read it, and said, 'Very well. Call him in next.'

The usher went out, and Bob muttered, 'The longer they talk, the worse it gets! They oughter just bring the little feller in and put him on the stand, and then everyone'd see he ain't a monster!'

'I don't think they will,' Joan whispered back. 'The longer it goes on, the more silly they'd look if they did. They just can't afford to now.'

The usher came to the court and announced, 'Dr Septimus Prosser, the Philosopher Royal!'

'Ah, they're all coming out the woodwork now,' said Bob under his breath, as the Philosopher Royal took the stand.

'What are your duties, Dr Prosser?' the lawyer began.

'His Majesty the King is a very gifted amateur philosopher. I have the honour to serve as his personal philosophical adviser.'

'Could you tell the court of your involvement with the Monster?'

'By all means. It came to my attention that there was a child who claimed he had been a rat. I was curious, so I traced the child and conducted some tests.'

Here the Philosopher Royal took some papers out of a briefcase and put on a pair of glasses.

'I found,' he went on, 'a remarkable degree of dissociation and denial, paranoid in nature. The creature's cognitive development was abnormally retarded . . .'

Bob was grinding his teeth. The Philosopher Royal talked smoothly on, explaining, demonstrating, defining, and Roger seemed to become less and less real, until he was only a word among a lot of other words.

Eventually the Judge interrupted, 'Dr Prosser, let me see if I understand you clearly. You maintain that the creature is essentially a rat, and not essentially a human?'

'Quite so, my lord. The intrinsic nature of the creature is such that there is no moral continuum between it and ourselves.'

'Again, let me try to clarify this. You maintain that we, as human beings, have no moral responsibility to this creature? It is not human, and therefore we should treat it as we might any kind of vermin?'

'Yes, that is the case.'

Bob could stand it no more. He stood and shook his fist at the Philosopher Royal, and roared, '*You* never treated him proper, you old fraud! You broke your word to us and you let him run away! Damn all this fancy talk! He ain't a monster or a creature or a rat or any kind of vermin – he's a little boy!'

The Judge was banging on the bench, the usher was hurrying towards Bob, two policemen were rushing in to help.

As they seized Bob's arm he shouted: 'Bring him to the court! Let 'em all have a look! Listen to him speak! Then you'll see! He's a little boy! He's human! He's like us! Bring him out and have a look at him!'

But they'd got him to the door by this time. Joan cried out to Bob that she was coming with him, but no-one could hear in all the confusion. People were shouting, jeering, laughing, standing on the benches to get a better look. It was the most exciting day in court for years.

The Daily Scourge

MONSTER CONDEMNED

The Monster of the Sewers is to die – official!

Yesterday, after sensational scenes at the Tribunal, the decision was handed down by the learned judge: **KILL THE FOUL BEAST**.

The Monster will be exterminated tomorrow.

CELEBRATIONS

There were wild scenes of joy outside the court when the verdict was announced.

Parents who had been keeping their children away from school celebrated with fireworks and street parties.

Seventy-eight people were injured, five of them seriously.

Our Philosophy Correspondent writes:

It was the testimony of Dr Prosser, the Philosopher Royal, that made the difference. **READ HIM TODAY**, only in the *Daily Scourge*.

THE PHILOSOPHER ROYAL SPEAKS – ONLY IN THE *SCOURGE!*

Don't believe in what you see!

by Dr Septimus Prosser

Wise men and women throughout the ages have said this again and again: appearances are deceptive.

It's not what something looks like on the surface that counts.

It's what lies underneath.

The Monster of the Sewers may look like a little child. He may have the appearance of a normal nine-year-old boy.

But how often have we been deceived by looks?

Our senses are limited things. We see very little compared to birds of prey. Next to bats, we're almost deaf. And as for the sense of smell, Fido and Rover have got us well beaten in that department.

SO WHO IS TO SAY THAT WE SHOULD TRUST THE APPEARANCE OF THIS CREATURE?

His true nature is what matters. Hidden, secret, dark, deceptive. A cesspool of wild appetites. That's the real truth of the matter.

Then there are those who ask what the Monster has 'done wrong'.

As if that matters!

Wrongness is in his very nature. It's what he is that matters, not what he does.

Philosophy says: **Don't trust your senses. The truth is not what you see. It's what you don't!**

SCARLET SLIPPERS, OR THE PRACTICAL VALUE OF CRAFTSMANSHIP

To tell the truth, the Philosopher Royal's article had been entirely rewritten by the sub-editor so the readers could understand it, but it was more or less what Dr Prosser had said.

Everyone agreed that this was a very effective article, and readers said to each other that of course you should never go by appearances, they never had done, you could never trust what someone looked like on the surface, they were bound to be different underneath.

Joan didn't read it, and nor did Bob. They were far too worried. After they'd been thrown out of the court, they had tried to find a reporter to tell their side of the story to, but no-one would listen. The

Daily Scourge had decided that the public was more interested in having the Monster exterminated, so that was that.

As the old couple sat that evening in despair about what they could do, Joan caught sight of the newspaper. Bob had thrown it down angrily after reading the philosophy article, and it had fallen in a heap, with one of the inside pages on top. On it was a picture of the new princess.

And something came to Joan's mind, and she said suddenly, 'Mary Jane!'

'Who's Mary Jane?' said Bob.

'D'you remember,' she said, gripping his arm, 'when we was talking about the royal wedding and the new Princess, Roger said she was really called Mary Jane!'

'Oh, aye, so he did. I thought he was just making up a yarn.'

'Well, so did I. But he was ever so firm about it, and it wasn't like him to be stubborn, so I didn't ask him any more – anyway,' she said, 'what about asking her to help?'

'How?' he said.

'I don't know. But she seems a nice kind person, to go by her picture—'

'Shouldn't go by appearances,' Bob said bitterly.

'Oh, that's philosophy. Common sense always

goes by appearances. I say she looks nice and she might *be* nice and it's the only thing we can do, isn't it?'

Bob scratched his head. 'Yeah,' he admitted, 'that's true enough.' Then he sat up. 'Here,' he said, 'I know how we can get to see her!'

'How?'

'You know them scarlet slippers I made, with the gold heels?'

She said nothing, but just looked at him, and nodded.

'Well,' he went on, 'we could take 'em to her as a present, and if she can't wear 'em herself she could use 'em for a royal child if one comes along. We'll go right away!'

PRINCESS MARY JANE

They knew the way to the palace well enough
by now, and they found the place much better
looked after than when they'd last come. There
were no high jinks in the servants' hall, no football
in the courtyard, no smoking in the sentry boxes.
Now the King and Queen were back from the Hotel
Splendifico, and the young Prince and Princess were
back from their honeymoon, everything was spick and
span and the servants were on their best behaviour.

The footman who came to answer their knock at
the tradesmen's entrance listened carefully, and
said, 'I shall convey your gift to Her Royal
Highness, and I'm sure her lady-in-waiting will
send you a note of thanks.'

'Could we see the Princess ourselves?' said Joan.
'It's really important, honest.'

'Not without an appointment, madam. Write to the Office of the Princess Aurelia at the Palace. Her Private Secretary will see to it.'

'But we *got* to see her!' said Bob, desperately. 'It's a matter of life and death!'

'I'm very sorry—' the footman began, but a voice behind him said:

'Who's this?'

It was a young lady's voice. The footman jumped with surprise, and bowed while he was still in mid-air, so he came down already in a crouch.

Bob and Joan could hardly believe their eyes. It was the new Princess herself, dressed in casual clothes, just standing there as ordinary as they were. The footman didn't know whether to fawn and grovel, or to tell her off for being in the wrong part of the Palace.

'Oh, Your Royal Highness,' said Joan quickly, 'we came to bring you a present—'

'How kind! Do come in,' she said.

The footman sagged with shock, but he had to go along with what the Princess wanted, and he held the door open for Bob and Joan.

They felt very shy. They followed the Princess along the corridor and up the stairs into a friendly-looking little sitting room, not at all grand and pompous like the rest of the palace.

'Er – here you are, Your Royal Highness,' said Bob, handing her the shoebox. 'If they don't fit, I expect they'll do one day for a littl'un. Beg your pardon – I mean a young princess. I made 'em meself,' he added.

'Oh, they're beautiful,' she said, kicking off the sandals she was wearing. 'And they fit me perfectly! Thank you so much. You're too kind.'

They did fit, too, small as they were. Bob could hardly believe his luck.

'I'm glad you like 'em, ma'am,' he said. 'But the thing is, we got a terrible problem – I don't like to impose, but we couldn't think of anyone else to ask—'

'Tell me about it,' she said. 'Let's sit down.'

She wasn't at all like you expected a princess to be, they agreed afterwards; just like a real person, in fact, but a thousand times prettier; and so kind and concerned. She listened to their story from the moment Bob heard the knock on the door to the moment they thought of bringing her the slippers.

The Princess listened wide-eyed, and didn't

speak till they'd finished. She'd gone pale.

'They're going to *kill* him?' she said.

'It's cruel and wicked,' said Bob, 'but we can't stop 'em. We done everything we could think of.'

'So we came to you,' said Joan, 'as a last resort, and I'm sorry to put this trouble on your doorstep, but the thing is, he said something about "Mary Jane", and—'

The Princess sat up sharply.

'But that's my name!' she said. 'Only no-one's supposed to know it. They said it wasn't a suitable name for a princess, and I had to change it. But tell me again: *when* did he say he changed into a boy?'

'He weren't sure,' said Bob, 'but reckoning backwards, I'd say it were just about the time your engagement was announced, ma'am.'

The Princess put her hand to her mouth.

'I know who he is!' she whispered. 'Please – don't ask any more – I'll help him,' she said. 'I'll do my best, I promise – but you mustn't ask me any more about it! Please! It's a deadly secret . . .'

'We wouldn't dream of betraying any secrets,' said Bob. 'And if you help to save that little boy, I'll keep you in

slippers for the rest of your life, ma'am.'

'Do you think you can, Your Royal Highness?' said Joan.

'I don't know what they'll let me do,' said the Princess, 'but I'll try my absolute hardest, I promise.'

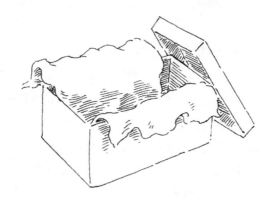

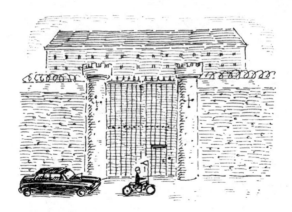

THE PRINCESS AND THE PRISON

Next day, the director of the quarantine department received an urgent message as soon as he arrived for work.

'Do not proceed with the E-programme for Subject No. 5463. Repeat, do not proceed. Expect Very Important Visitor. Make sure Subject is clean and presentable.'

The director was very relieved. E stood for extermination, and he hadn't been looking forward to it. He gave orders for Subject No. 5463 to be washed and placed in a comfortable cage, and then he got ready for his Very Important Visitor, having no idea who it could be, of course.

When his secretary announced in a trembly voice, 'Her Royal Highness the Princess Aurelia,' he nearly fainted.

Like everyone else, he was fascinated by the graceful and charming princess. He'd read all the accounts of her whirlwind engagement, he'd been among the crowd cheering on the wedding day, he'd half-fallen in love with her himself, as so many others had done. To find her here, in his own office, almost made him dizzy.

She was wearing something that made her look even prettier than he could imagine. There was a detective to guard her and a lady-in-waiting to accompany her, and through all the bewildered roaring in his ears the director heard her say something about the Rat-Boy.

'I'm sorry,' he said, 'the . . . did you say . . .?'

'Yes,' she said, 'I'd like to visit him if I may.'

'He's – er – very dangerous, ma'am,' he managed to say. 'He doesn't look it but, as you know, appearances are very deceptive. It's easy to be misled into thinking he's harmless, but—'

'Yes, I understand,' she said. 'But I'm very interested in this case, and I'd like to see for myself.'

'Of course! By all means! Now we'll just call three or four

keepers – they'll be armed, don't worry – and then I'll take you along to his cage.'

'Why do you keep him in a cage?' said the Princess.

'Because he is a being of unknown origin, something sinister and dangerous,' the director explained patiently. She was so pretty, he thought, it didn't matter if she wasn't very clever.

'I see,' she said. 'Well, I'd like to see him anyway. And if he's in a cage, I won't need any other protection.'

She was stubborn too. She wouldn't agree to the armed member of staff, and she insisted on her lady-in-waiting and her detective staying in the office. She wanted to see the Monster alone, and that was that.

Well, she was the Princess, and they had to agree, although the idea of this fragrant delicate beauty face to face with the ravening Monster of the Sewers made the director shiver. It was too horrible to think about what might happen, so he tried not to think about anything, and ordered some coffee and made conversation with the lady-in-waiting instead.

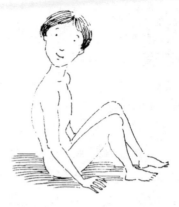

WISH AS HARD AS YOU LIKE

Roger was sitting on the floor of his cage counting his toes, when the door of the room opened and someone came in. He didn't look up; they were all the same, except that some of them were worse.

But his nostrils caught a nice smell, like flowers.

It reminded him of something. He twitched a bit harder – and then he looked up.

'Mary Jane!' he cried.

She was alone. He jumped up with delight, never minding that he hadn't got any clothes on, and ran to reach out through the bars.

She took his hands.

'Hush, Ratty,' she said, 'you mustn't call me Mary Jane any more. We both been changed, and you're Roger now, isn't that right? Well, I'm Princess

Aurelia. So you mustn't tell anyone about Mary Jane, and I won't tell anyone you were a rat.'

'I kept telling 'em,' he said, 'only no-one believed me! First they never believed I was a rat, then they never believed I'm a boy! I don't understand 'em, truly I don't.'

'Bob and Joan came to see me last night,' she said. 'I never knew about any of it till then. Oh, they're so worried about you, Roger. And I told them I'd help, and I'll try, truly I will. It's horrible what these people are doing to you, it's wrong and wicked, and I'll get it stopped, see if I don't. Evil monster from the sewers! I never heard such nonsense!'

'Where's the monster?' said Roger, half-frightened.

'There isn't one,' she said. 'Now listen carefully, because we might not be able to talk again like this, in private I mean. What do you remember about being a rat?'

'Well, I was a little boy rat, and we lived near the cheese stall in the market, just behind your house. And you used to work in the kitchen. And you used to give me scraps and tickle me and call me Ratty. I remember that now, but I forgot it before. Then one day you caught me in a shoebox and brung me in the kitchen too, and before I knew anything else, I was a boy, standing up like this, only with clothes on.'

'Do you remember what changed you?'

'No. When I was a rat I didn't know anything, and when I was a boy it was all over already. But you was all dressed up for dancing, and I had to go with you on the coach and open the door and pull the step down and go with you into the palace. This beautiful lady told me all that, and I done it.'

'And you were supposed to wait with the coach for me to come back.'

'Was I? That must be what I forgot to do. Yes, I remember! I got lost in the palace and got up to mischief. Me and the palace page-boys, we played football in them long corridors upstairs, and we slid down the banisters, and we crept in the kitchen and ate the jellies and sausage rolls. We done all kinds of things. And then I was supposed to go back on the coach, and put the step up after you and shut the door and all, only when I remembered and went

166

there, you was gone and there wasn't a coach or nothing. And they wouldn't let me back in the palace because all them other page-boys had been whipped and sent to bed, and I didn't belong, I had the wrong uniform, so they sent me away.

'And after that I dunno what I done. All kinds of bad things, I think. Then I found Bob and Joan, only I got lost again, and now I'm in prison. I think they're going to sterminate me, Mary Jane, and if Bob and Joan knew about it, they wouldn't let it happen. Maybe it'd be best if I went back to being a proper rat. I tried being a rat in the sewers, only nothing went right. I can't go back and I can't go forward, I don't know what to do, Mary Jane, really I don't. Can I go back?'

'I don't reckon you can,' she said, 'any more than I can. You're stuck as a boy, and I'm stuck as a princess.'

'Don't you want to be a princess, Mary Jane?'

'Well, I did to start with. I longed for it. I wished so hard! But I'm not sure any more. I'm so afraid I made a mistake, Roger. I might have been better off staying as Mary Jane. See, I don't think it's what you *are* that matters. I think it's what you *do*. I think they'd like me to just *be*, and not do anything. That's the trouble.'

'We oughter work that magic again, like what changed us in the first place,' he said.

'I wish we could,' she said.

'We could try and wish that lady back!'

'Yes,' she said, 'let's try.'

She was holding his hands through the bars. The Princess and the Monster closed their eyes and wished, as hard as they could, till they were

trembling with it; but when they opened their eyes, nothing had changed, and the only beautiful lady there was the Princess herself.

'Well, perhaps we can't,' she said after a moment or two. 'It goes to show. Maybe she only comes once, and grants you a wish, and then you're stuck with the consequences. I suppose we'll have to make the best of it.'

'Well, I *could* go on being a boy,' said Roger, 'if only they'd let me. I can do it quite well most of the time, except when they make out I'm something else underneath.'

'We'll have to see what we can do,' said the Princess.

The Daily Scourge

MIRACLE OF PRINCESS AND 'MONSTER'

There were extraordinary scenes yesterday outside the Palace as the news emerged of Princess Aurelia's miracle intervention in the so-called 'Monster' case.

As many had suspected, the 'Monster' was nothing of the sort.

A FAIRY-TALE PRINCESS

It took the clear-sighted vision of a fairy-tale Princess to penetrate to the heart of the matter, and see the astounding truth:

THE MONSTER WAS ONLY A LITTLE BOY.

Not a subhuman fiend. Not a venom-dripping beast from the nethermost pit of hell.

Just a normal little fellow like any other. Mischievous, perhaps – but evil?

Not in a month of Sundays!

LUCKY TO BE ALIVE

The boy is to be released into the care of foster-parents, and apprenticed to a decent trade.

THE SCOURGE SAYS:

GOD BLESS PRINCESS AURELIA!
There's no corner of the world so dark that a little ray of magic from a Princess's heart can't light it up.

As for these self-appointed 'experts' and 'philosophers':
WHERE IS THEIR COMPASSION?
Thanks to Princess Aurelia, a little boy can sleep safe tonight.

How many more innocent children are under threat from our cruel cold-hearted system of so-called justice?

Princess or angel?

THE POWER OF THE PRESS

On every front page of every newspaper in the country there were big pictures of the Princess, looking beautiful and concerned, and the stories that went with them were confusing, but they all said roughly the same thing: the Princess, by the superhuman power of her love and compassion, had worked a miracle and transformed the ghastly evil ravening Monster of the Sewers into a normal little boy.

What had really happened, of course, was simple. The *Daily Scourge* had seen an even better story than the one about the Monster of the Sewers. The Princess Aurelia story had everything, and it could run for years, with prettier pictures, too.

TOASTED CHEESE

'Well, I never knew the like,' said Bob. 'I tell you this, I'm fed up with them blooming papers. I'll never buy one again.'

'Yes you will,' said Joan. 'You'll buy it for the sports and the crossword, and then you'll just see what's happened in the news, and you'll believe it just as much as you ever did.'

'I won't,' he said, but he didn't want to argue.

In the corner, Roger was busy stitching a little shoe. He hardly ever nibbled the leather any more, and Bob could leave his beeswax on the bench and only find two or three toothmarks when he came back.

'Look,' said the boy. 'Is that neat? I think it is. I stitched it ever so tight all the way round.'

'Just right,' said Bob, peering through his glasses. 'I reckon you're going to be a good cobbler.'

'Roger, love,' said Joan, 'come here a minute. I want to ask you something.'

The little boy came and stood on the hearth in front of her. He had new clothes on, and his brown hair was neatly brushed, and his black eyes shone.

'Yes?' he said politely.

'What really happened when the Princess came and saw you?' she said. 'All this stuff about miracles and so on. No-one's told us the truth, and no-one ever will unless you do.'

'We just talked,' said Roger. 'And she remembered who I was, because she used to know me when I was a rat. Then I was made into a page-boy when she went to the Ball, only I missed the coach back through getting up to mischief. If I'd gone back on that coach I'd've been made back into a rat. I suppose that might have been better, except I might have remembered being a boy and I'd've wanted to be a boy again, for ever.

'But she's changed too now, Mary Jane has. I mean the Princess. She ain't so happy now. It all come about because of her wish, and that goes to show,' he said.

'What's it go to show?' said Bob.

'I dunno. It's what she said. But she made me promise to be as good a boy as I could, and she promised me she was going to be as good a princess as she could, and that was the consequence.'

'Ah,' said Bob. 'And do you want to be a rat now?'

'It'd be easier,' said Roger. 'You have less trouble being a rat, except for being sterminated. I wouldn't want that. It's hard being a person, but it's not so hard if they think you *are* a person. If they think you ain't a person, then it's too hard for me. I think I'll stick to cobbling.'

'That's a wise decision,' said Bob. 'There's always a demand for good craftsmanship. If I hadn't made them slippers, well, I don't like to think what would have happened.'

The kettle came to the boil, so Joan made them all a cup of tea, and Bob toasted some cheese, and they all sat down comfortably around the hearth. The world outside was a difficult place, but toasted cheese and love and craftsmanship would do to keep them safe.